Milestones

By Rhett Smith

Dedications:

For my family for laughing at me.
For Alice for putting up with me.
And for my nan and Grandad who have always reminded me to live.

All rights reserved
Copyright © Rhett Smith 2024

Published by A1 Book Publishing UK

The right of Rhett Smith to be identified as the author of this work has been asserted in accordance with Section 789 of the Copyright, Designs, and Patents Act 1988

This book is sold subject to the conditions that it shall not, by way of trade or otherwise, be lent, resold, hired out or otherwise circulated without the author's prior consent in any form of binding or cover other than that in which it is published and without a similar condition including this condition being imposed on the subsequent purchaser.

ISBN 9798327660007

Prologue

Our lives are shaped by the choices we make. The ones that are within our control are easier to comprehend. We can weigh up the pros and cons of a decision, and if it doesn't go according to plan, we can put it down to poor judgment. The little choices we make, the ones we have no idea how they are going to pan out, are more difficult. We just have to go with it and rely on blind faith. And then there are the choices that other people make for you. Those choices we have no control over. They are the ones that can turn your life completely upside down. And that's exactly what happened.

1. Saturday Nights Alright For Fighting

Saturday, February 3rd, 2024.

I watch as Michelle scrapes every last ounce of mint choco chip ice cream from her bowl. I wait patiently for her to finish, so I can take them away. I put the bowls in the sink and wash them up. I can't stand to see dirty pots sitting on the side for more than a minute. I hear her shout through the sound of running water, "I want more," she says.
 "I'm sorry, I didn't quite hear you," I reply, moving towards the door separating the kitchen and the living room.
"I said I want more."
"There's none left," I reply, that was the last of it.
"I would go out and get some more, but it's 11 o'clock on a Saturday night, and we've had a bottle of wine each."
She looks at me deadly serious. "I mean, I want more than this. Me and you, I don't want to be with you anymore."
When you've been with someone for 12 years, you can tell when they're joking, and it didn't seem as if she was. "Is this a joke? Because if it is, it's not a very funny one," I say, a little annoyed.
"Robert, this isn't a joke!" The use of my full name confirms that it isn't, "nor is it a spur-of-the-moment thing. I've been thinking about this for a while now."
I look at her puzzled. "I didn't realize you were unhappy?" I reply, snappier than I want it to sound.
"I wouldn't say I was unhappy," she says, the resentment in her voice softening slightly.
"Then please explain."
 "Well, it's like this. We've been together since we were 16. I'm 28 years old now, and you're the only man I've been with. You went off to Cambridge and got a degree, while I spent my best years working for my parents and waiting for you to come home to visit. I meet up with my friends, and they tell me all these stories of the

lives they've lived, the places they've been, and the things they've done. Amanda has been married three times; once was in Vegas. Jennifer has just come back from traveling Europe, and Veronica is seeing a 21-year-old fitness instructor."

I see a gap and take my chance, "So what you're saying is that you're leaving me because your friends have fucked up every relationship they've ever had, and you want to be like them." I was angry now.

"No, Rob. What I'm saying is the only excitement I get is when the Chinese takeaway gives us 11 chicken balls instead of 10. I want to see the world. I want to have a one-night stand with a French man. I want to drink way too much and throw up in the canals of Amsterdam. When my dad died 2 years ago, he left me 10 grand in his will. I didn't want to tell you about it because I didn't want it to be used for some sort of renovation of the house. I'm going to use the money to go traveling with Jennifer. I'll figure the rest out as I go along. You can have the house; it's only a rental. And my two-nights-a-week job at the chip shop wasn't really contributing that much anyway."

"Wow!" I say when she's finished.

"What does "wow" mean? Say what you're thinking, Rob!" she demands.

"Well, first of all, "wow" as in that's a whole lot of information to take in all at once. And secondly, aren't you a little bit young to have a midlife crisis? Can't you buy a motorbike or take up golf instead?" I ask, managing the smallest of smiles.

"I'm serious, Rob. This is happening." I go back into the kitchen, open the fridge, and take out another bottle of red wine. After uncorking it, I pour myself a glass and returned to the living room. I walk past her to the sofa opposite.

"What are you doing?" she says, looking confused.

"Well, before I take any more of a battering, I need something to soften the blow. Please continue."

She looks at me like I'm a bird who can't fly anymore because I've hurt my wings. "I love you, Rob, and I always will. This is just something I have to do. I don't want to look back on my life and regret the things I haven't done."

It takes all my resolve not to cry. It's like holding in a sneeze when you're going 100 mph down the motorway. One false move and it's all over. It's not that I'm ashamed to cry in front of her, it's more that I don't want her to win. The other thing I don't want to do is rile her up. I feel like after finishing off the wine in my glass, there's every chance that will happen. So I regroup and sit there, thinking of a game plan.

"Ok," I say, "If that's really what you want, then there's nothing I can do to stop you. I'm going to go up to bed. Are you coming?"

"I'm going to stay up for a while," she replies.

You see, my plan is to leave her with her own thoughts, let her second-guess herself. Perhaps she will feel a bit guilty. Maybe she will sleep on it, and then in the morning, it will be forgotten. I brush my teeth and climb into bed. The alcohol helps me doze off within minutes. I don't hear or feel her climb into bed next to me.

The next day, I wake up to the sound of the back door slamming. My head is pounding and my mouth is dry. I seriously regret that last glass of wine. *Michelle is probably taking the empty bottles of wine out to the recycling*, I think to myself as I lay there nursing my head. The events of last night hit me like a bolt of lightning. I have no idea how this morning is going to play out. Hopefully, she will come into the bedroom, looking sheepish, bearing a cup of tea as an apology. I will tell her to forget it ever happened, to put the cup of tea down and join me under the covers. It is until I hear the sound of the garage door opening and the wheels of a suitcase against the concrete, that I know that isn't going to happen. The bedroom door opens. She enters the room and starts unloading her possessions into the large suitcase.

"Michelle, don't do this," I say, trying not to sound desperate.

"I've told you, Rob, it's happening. Now, can you please get out of bed so I can finish packing?" she replies. I do as I'm told and go downstairs to make that cup of tea myself. 15 minutes later, she enters the kitchen. The wheels of the suitcase reverberate against the expensive laminate flooring she just had to have. "Where are you going to stay then?" I ask.

"France," she replies.

"Is it that bad that you're leaving the country?" I say, only half-joking.

"Don't be funny, Rob. You know my mum lives out there."

"Well, I suppose I'll hate you less if I don't see you around," I snap.

"Come on, Rob. That's not fair," she snaps back.

"Fair? You want to talk about fair, Michelle? Do you think it's fair that you're about to throw away a 12-year relationship because you're bored? When most people are bored, they take up running or go to the cinema. They don't just get up and leave. Also, I don't ever recall you mentioning anything about holidays, restaurants, or day trips to the coast. You were happy, just like I was, to get a takeaway, put your feet up, and watch a film,"

She doesn't say anything. She just takes her keys out of her pocket, removes both the front and back doors from the keyring, places them on the counter, and turns to leave.

"Michelle, wait!" I shout. She turns to face me. "I'll do it. I'll do it all. Well, not the one-night stand with the Frenchman, that would be weird. But if you want to throw up in the canals of Amsterdam, I will hold your hair back while you do. You want to go skinny dipping in the Mediterranean Sea? I'll strip off and join you. I love you, Michelle. Please don't go."

My face starts to dampen, and I realize I'm crying. She looks at me like she's almost contemplating staying. I have her on the ropes.

But then she deals the knockout blow. "Rob, I'm not in love with you anymore."

My heart sinks because that's when I realize that it's pointless. Everything I do or say now, is pointless.

"I'm sorry," she adds.

"Ok. If that's how you feel, I suppose I've got no choice but to let you go." I say, admitting defeat.

"Thank you." She replies. As if I've done her a massive favour. "I know this is going to sound condescending, but you're going to be fine." I just nod with a mixed feeling of a hangover and being mentally drained. There's nothing left to say.

"Goodbye, Rob." She says softly and walks out the door. I stand there in the silent empty kitchen, and think to myself what now? The afternoon and the evening seem to merge into one. One minute, time seems to stand still, the next it propels. It's funny. I've lived with Michelle since we were 22 years old. And in that time, we've never spent a night away from each other.

We become so dependent on the company of others that when we're alone, we forget how to truly live. I make pie and chips, far too many chips. I uncork a bottle of wine and instinctively fill two glasses. Having the full control of TV, I end up watching the same things that I would've watched with her. After three glasses of wine,

I do the thing I promised myself I wouldn't do. I pick up my phone and call her number. Straight to voicemail, I thought as much. The robotic voice asks me to leave my message so I do. "Hi Michelle. It's Rob. I just wanted to say, I wish you the very best in your endeavours and hope you live a happy life. You're probably at the airport. If you are, I hope your plane gets delayed. And if you're already on the plane, I hope your in-flight meal is shit." The voice is back, asking me if I want to send the message. I think, why not? She won't listen to it anyway, so I send it. I down the last remnants of the now warm red wine in the bottom of the glass before taking myself to bed. Tomorrow will be a new day.

2. Jesus Lives At Kings Cross Station

The alarm goes off at 7.00. I tiptoe my way out of bed, like every morning, before realizing that the person I'm trying not to wake has fucked off to France and left me. Opening my wardrobe I take out a pair of trousers, a shirt, and my best work tie, Catching my reflection in the mirror of the wardrobe door as it closes. Today is the biggest day of my career so far and my face looks like I've spent the night in a cement mixer. My line of work is advertising for an aftershave company called Amato's, which has 2 branches: the main branch in Rome and a second branch in London. Well, Leicester Square to be precise. I work at the Leicester Square one, which is really handy, because it would be a hell of a commute to Rome every day. If you think of Paco Rabanne as Marks and Spencer, Amato wouldn't be Tesco's. It wouldn't even be Aldi. It's more like Poundland.

But everything could be about to change, as Amato's has secured an investor—a major company looking to launch an entirely new line of aftershaves to rival the big guns. The project includes a TV advertisement, which is where I come in. And that's why, today is a big day. I've got a meeting with the boss. Not Luca Amato himself, but my boss Steve Smith. The most British name in history. He's a straight-shooting kind of guy. His dad was in the army, so believes every man should be as tough as he is. He's a father of two, watched both of his kids being born, yet the only time he's ever shed a tear was when Arsenal won the FA Cup.

In order to impress him, I can't show any vulnerability. So, Michelle's leaving couldn't have come at a worse time. I hadn't mentioned the meeting to her, not wanting to jinx it. Then something she said the night she was leaving strikes me: she had 10 grand in the bank and never mentioned it. Sure, it was her money, and she had every right to do what she wanted with it. But watching me exhaust myself, falling asleep on the sofa night after

night, and never offering to help—that was a bit shitty. But I need to let this go or it could end up sabotaging my meeting.
I put the kettle on and get 2 slices of bread out of the bread bin. I need food. Seeing the mould on the bread, I realize I'm going to have to grab something on the way. I sit down at the kitchen table and open up my briefcase, carefully going over my proposal. I look at the time, 7.40 am. Need to go. Swigging the lukewarm tea, I leave the house.

I head towards King's Cross Tube Station. The weather is mild, and the London streets are already bustling with commuters. My stomach growls at me. I spot a Gregg's and think that's going to have to do. I'll get a sausage roll to tide me over. I enter the store and take my place in the queue. "Who's next, please?" bellows a lad no older than 20.
I walk to the counter. "Just a sausage roll, please," I say politely.
"Eat in or takeaway?" he asks.
"Um, takeaway please," I reply.
"£1.45, then, please," he says. I hand over the money and make my way to the exit. I spot a newspaper on one of the tables on the way out. *Fuck it* I think to myself. I will sit in. It's been ages since I've sat and read a paper. I take a seat.
"Excuse me," Says the lad who served me. "You can't sit there."
"Why not? Nobody's sitting here," I ask.
"I know," He replies. "But you've paid to take away. To eat in is another 30p."
"What? How come?" I ask, gobsmacked.
"I don't know. I don't make the rules," he answers.
"But that's ridiculous," I laugh.
"Look buddy, my girlfriend's pregnant!" he snaps.
"What's that got to do with anything," I reply, even more confused.
"She's struggling to sleep, which means I'm struggling to sleep, which means I'm tired, which means I don't have the energy, to have a conversation with someone who doesn't know Gregg's rules."

He says Gregg's, like Gregg is a bloke who works alongside him and has nipped out and left him in charge.
"Can't you just let me sit here?" I say.
"I can't, I'm afraid. I'm already on my final warning for nicking the sauce sachets. One more strike and I'm out, So, either pay the 30p or leave," he says with the limited authority he possesses.
"Okay, I'll leave," I say. And I do.

Kings Cross Station is a playground for weirdos. Two supposedly homeless men, with newer smartphones than me, ask me for a pound. And as I'm just about to bite into my sausage roll, a long-haired man in a suede jacket stops me. "Do you know that Jesus died for you to be able to enjoy that sausage roll?" he exclaims.
"Really?" I reply, "Well, can you thank him for me? I've lost his phone number," I say, playing along.
"You just did," he replies. "For I am he."
I realize I haven't got time for this. "Well, Jesus, could you do me a favour and get a job like the rest of us? Because you're stopping me from getting to mine," I reply. Then he bows to me like a karate student greeting his sensei before allowing me past.
I make my way underground following the signs for the Piccadilly line, and stand at the platform ready to get on the tube. I fish my headphones out of my bag in preparation to block out the absolute chaos of the London underground. I put my headphones in and press shuffle. The song is "Badly Drawn Boy", "What Is It Now", from the album "Have You Fed the Fish".
And the lyrics are:
"So now that life will never be the same.
We've got to face the thought of loneliness again."
I have to laugh at the irony of the song. Some people would say it's fated that this particular song would come on. Especially with what's happened over the past few days. But I don't believe in fate. I believe that life is a series of coincidences linked together to trick you into thinking fate exists.

The tube arrives. I join the stampede of people, fighting for space. Luckily for me, the Leicester Square stop isn't far. I grab the pole and get pushed, so far into it that I nearly eat it. The song changes and it's Guy Garvey and Richard Hawley singing about rigging a horse race, which doesn't resonate with me at all, but it's a cracking song. I get off at my stop and walk up to the already crowded Leicester Square. I walk past the souvenir shops, the stalls selling cheap theatre tickets, the IMAX cinema, and the **four-story M&M store**. Which has always baffled me. Is M&M's popular enough to have a **four-floor store**? Apparently so. I swing left down a couple of side streets to a long thin building that is Amato's. Clive, the security guard, has already set up shop. He's a rotund bloke with a bald head. Think more of Phil Mitchell than Jason Statham. I sometimes envy bald people. They must save a fortune on haircuts. I've never understood why we've needed a security guard. It's not as if it's Wonka's Chocolate Factory. What are people going to do, break-in, steal a sample, run it through a test lab, and make their own aftershave?

"Morning, Clive," I say as he gets the door for me. I climb the stairs to the offices. The space is one big oval with Steve's office slap bang in the middle and the rest of the tiny little offices around the sides, including mine. He's purposely done this so he can keep an eye on everyone with just a swivel of his chair. I make my way to my office. Luckily, it's not directly in his eyesight.

My office is simplistic. There's no stress ball, no motivational poster that says things like, "You can do this" or "Go hard or go home." I have my desk and a few file cabinets, and that's about it. On my desk, there's a picture of me and Michelle at a friend's wedding. With her, dyed red hair and nose piercing, and my bedhead hair, we look like the front cover of the NME.

I put the picture in the bottom drawer of the cabinet, its too distracting. The clock on the wall shows 8.40 am. Nerves are starting to get the better of me. I could do with a drink to calm myself but this isn't Mad Men and I am no Don Draper. I'm just about to go over my proposal one more time when my phone rings. It's my mum. I have to answer it. What if it's an emergency? "Hi Mum,"

"I'm sorry to hear about you and Michelle, darling," she says, sympathetically.

"How do you know about that?" I ask, confused.

"Facebook," she says, like it was obvious. "She's changed her relationship status to single. What happened?"

"We wanted different things, Mum."

"What kind of things?" she asks, poking further. *Well, she wants to sleep with other men and I don't* is what I want to say but think better of it. "I'll explain another time," I say.

"Well, I know just the thing that will cheer you up."

"What's that?" I ask, holding no hope.

"Some of my famous homemade chili. I know it's your favourite."

"You don't have to go through the trouble of making that for me, Mum," I say, bursting her balloon.

"Don't be silly, There's loads left over. I made too much. Me and your dad couldn't finish it. I'll give it to you next time you come round. Speaking of which, are you still coming on Sunday?"

"Yes, Mum. Do you need me to bring anything?" I answer,

"No, just yourself. Actually, can you pick up the pudding? Jam roly-poly and custard. But not the supermarket one, I don't like that one. Oh, and some of those sausages your dad likes. He will play hell with me if he knows you're coming and I didn't get you to bring some," she adds.

"Is that it, Mum? Anything else?" I say, trying to wrap up the conversation.

"Yes. Oh, one more thing, can you pick me up a potato peeler? Ours is broken," she answers.

"Pudding, sausages, potato peeler. Got it. Right, Mum, I've got to go. I'm about to start work," I say, really pressed for time now.

"Okay, darling, I love you. Have a good day and keep your chin up." She says.

"Love you too, mum," I reply, before hanging up.

At 8.59, I make my way to my boss's office. He sees me through the glass and holds up a finger to say hang on one minute. He's on the phone and he's very animated. I can't hear what's being said but he doesn't look happy. He's a bald, thickset man, with a black and white moustache. As i watch him talk I start to panic that my proposal isn't good enough, or maybe he's already selected the people for the job and my interview is just a formality. He puts the phone down and motions me in.

"Sorry about that," He says, as he shuffles some papers, "That was my ex-wife. Apparently, letting my 6-year-old daughter watch the Saw films is bad parenting. This coming from a woman who, when the midwife handed her our pale white daughter with fire-red hair and asked her what we were going to call her, she replied, 'I quite like the name Shaniqua.' *Huh* ... Right anyway, Rob," he continues, "You've been with us for 6 years, and I can't fault your work. But up until now, you've only worked solo. This opportunity is a big one, and if we decide to go with you, you will be working with three other people. Now, we need someone fully committed. Someone who can work as a team and can compromise with others. So, when you're ready, the floor is yours." He says it like it's an X-Factor audition.

I take a seat. And I'm just about to open my briefcase when I freeze. It hits me that Michelle has left, and she isn't coming back. It has finally sunk in. I am completely alone for the first time ever. *Is this a good idea? Can I give this job my complete undivided attention? Am I in the right mindset for it?*

"Rob? Rob? Hello, Rob?" Steve says, trying to snap me out of my apprehension. "Is everything okay?" he asks.

Snapping out of my thoughts, I decide to be honest with him. "Not really," I say. "Michelle has left me."

He looks at me for a minute, his brow furrowing, deciding my fate. "What are the chances of her coming back?" he asks.

"Very slim," I reply, trying not to sound too pathetic.

"Well, that's fantastic news," he almost yells. "Well, obviously not for you. You must be devastated. But for the job, it's brilliant. I don't need to hear your proposal; the job is yours," he finishes.

Is this a dream? What is happening here? "I'm not sure I follow," I say, confused.

"Look, Rob, it's like this," he begins. "I've been working in advertising for a long time, and in my personal experience, the best candidates for the big jobs are single people. Because they have nobody to go home to, fewer commitments, more likely to stay late, and more likely to roll their sleeves up and get stuck in. I know it's harsh, but it's true. We don't want someone who can't stay late because it's their partner's birthday, and they are taking them out for a meal. Or someone who can't make it in at 9:00 because they've got to do the school run. We already know you're good at your job. Today was more about whether or not you can handle the workload. And I'm pretty confident you can. So congratulations, Rob, it's yours."

At that moment, I really don't know what to say, so I just say "Thank you", shake his hand, and leave. I get back to my office and try to comprehend what has just happened. I feel a fluttering of nerves and excitement swirling around in my stomach like a cocktail. I slide my phone out of my pocket and dial the one person I would have been excited to tell 3 days ago. Voicemail again. "Hello Michelle, it's me again. I just wanted to say that I have just landed the biggest deal of my career so far. Not like you care. Anyway, I hope the airline has lost your luggage. Have a nice vacation. Bye."

I'm not sure what these voicemail messages are going to achieve. Maybe, I think she will have a change of heart and come back. Or maybe, I just want her to know that I'm going to move on with my life. But one thing I do know after the last two days, today is a win.

3. If your right hand is causing you pain, cut it off!

Sunday 11th of February 2024

In this scenario, the right hand that is causing me pain is all the things Michelle bought for the house, that I hate. So I spend the week cutting it off by getting rid of it. Starting with the ugly pea-green leather sofa that sticks to you in the summer and is absolutely freezing in the winter. And replacing it with a simple grey fabric 2-seated sofa and the armchair to go with it. I take down all the pictures of us together and replace them with a few movie posters I've had framed. In the living room, there's now a picture of Matt Damon and Robin Williams sitting on the hood of a car from Goodwill Hunting. And in the kitchen is now a picture of Bruce Lee wielding a pair of nun chucks from Enter the Dragon. I even went out and bought a proper bookcase and fetched all my books (that were apparently taking up too much room) from out of the garage. I arranged them in an order of favourite authors, with David Nicholls, Ian McEwan, and Haruki Murakami taking gold, silver, and bronze. I even succumbed to the global popularity of owning an air fryer. With Michelle gone, cooking seems like a lot of time and effort, just to eat alone.

Sunday comes round and I pick up the things mum has asked me to bring for Sunday dinner. And put them in a bag. Before making my way to the tube station. The wind blusters, it's like walking uphill. Mum and Dad live in Watford which is a 33-minute tube ride from Kings Cross. I've never listened to an audiobook. I'm old school. I like the feel and the smell of a paperback. But trying to read on the tube when it's match day and one of the many London teams is playing is nearly impossible. So, I downloaded an audiobook and put on my headphones, I thought I was going to get some clunky robotic voice. But what I actually got was a bloke with all the excitement of a children's TV presenter. He even changed his voice for the different characters, I'm so invested that when the tube comes to my stop, I don't want to turn it off.

I make the small walk to my mum and dad's **house**. I've already filled my mum in on what's happened between me and Michelle earlier in the week, leaving a few bits out. One thing about your parents; if you share something bad that your partner has said or done, you might find it in your heart to forgive them, but they won't. They will never forget it either.
My mum's grey-haired, furrowed forehead pops around the door to greet me as she sees me walking up the long cobbled driveway. The rest of her 5ft 4in slim frame emerges and gives me a hug. My parents house is old-fashioned, yet lovely. They have a proper log fire and a long oak dining table surrounded by several china cabinets. The kitchen has an island and a breakfast bar. The whole thing is so nicely decorated.
I follow Mum into the kitchen and put the bag down on the island. "Where's Dad?" I ask. As the words leave my mouth, we hear a knock at the door and the sound of my dad running down the stairs. "Cheers mate," we hear him say as the door slams behind him. He comes through the living room and into the kitchen. Being 6ft 3in, he has to duck slightly. I see the crown of his silver head, then see the rest of his bulky frame that years of being a builder has made him. "It's here," he cries excitedly. "All twelve inches of it."
"Graham!" my mum shouts. "What on earth have you ordered?"
"Jesus Christ, woman!" he shouts back. "It's a 12-inch vinyl for my record collection. Calm down, will you?"
"Calm down!" She shouts back, "If I came into the kitchen with a parcel and said, 'Here it is, all twelve inches of it,' I think you might react the same way."
"OK, point taken," he replies, defeated.
"Now make yourself useful and **make** Rob a cup of tea," she demands.

"You make him a cup of tea, I've got something I want to show him."

"Is it ready?" I ask, forcing a smile. He's nodding his head with a smile that reminds me of a serial killer you see in the films. I follow him out to the garden, which looks like the Chelsea Flower Show, filled with hydrangeas and geraniums. One of the perks of being retired is that you have all the time in the world to maintain the things that need maintaining. He presses the button on a key fob. The garage door tilts open. For weeks, nobody has been able to go near this garage. And now, what was once a hoarder's paradise is now a library of books and vinyls. At least, 7 full-length shelves hug the walls. There's a turntable and a recliner chair in one of the corners. And a small table with a kettle.

"Has Mum kicked you out?" I say, with a wry smile before realizing it's a bad joke considering my own situation.

"No," he chuckles lightly. "I need somewhere to go when your mum has her book club round. You want to see it, Rob. It's chaos. There are five of them, all over 60. They drink wine like it's going out of fashion. The more they drink, the more passionate about the book they become, and the louder they become. It's like an episode of The Real Housewives of Orange County. One month, they read Fifty Shades of Grey, and one of the women, Dorothy, loved it. She's 74. One woman only drinks red wine, one only drinks gin. And one of them is allergic to fish, which your mother only found out after bringing out a tray of tuna sandwiches. So I just come in here out of the way. I make myself a nice cup of tea. And put a record on," he finishes.

"Sounds good, Dad," I say with a slight twinge of envy.

"Anyway, how are you holding up?" he asks.

"I don't know, Dad, to be honest with you, I just miss her. The house is so empty. I go about my day and I'm fine. But then something will happen that will either remind me of her or I want to tell her about it and she's not there. I just can't shake the feeling that I could've done more to make her happier."

"Well, from what your mother's told me, I don't think there was anything you could have done," he sees my face fill with disdain. "Look, Rob," he begins, placing a hand on my shoulder. "Let me give you a piece of advice that I learned a little bit too late. Don't waste energy on the things you have no control over. If you make a mistake, fine, you can beat yourself up or go over the things you could have done differently. It still won't help, but we all do it. But if something happens to you that isn't your fault or your choice, then there's not really a lot you can do."

"Thanks, Dad," I say, and I genuinely mean it.

"Right, I'm going to put this record on because I've been waiting weeks for it to arrive." He says excitedly. He puts the record on the turntable and places the needle on the record. The static play is followed by the jangling guitar of Johnny Marr. The album is "Meat is Murder" by "The Smiths" and Morrissey is singing about the corporal punishment of the British School System. After a few more songs, Mum comes to the garage to tell us dinner is ready and we follow her back into the house.

I take my seat at the table and help myself to the plate of beef. I take three medium-sized pieces and add them to my plate of veggies and Yorkshire puddings before drowning it all in gravy.

"Do you think people from Yorkshire just call them puddings?" Dad asks as he opens two bottles of crafted ale and places one next to me.

"Graham, what are you talking about?" my mum scolds.

"We call them Yorkshire puddings. But if you're from Yorkshire, would you just call them puddings? Like shepherd's pie. Do shepherds just call it pie?"

"Ignore your father, Rob. He does this all the time. He must have heard this at the golf club and thought to himself, 'I like that, I'm going to use that one.'"

I laugh for the first time in days. "Thank you for making dinner, Mum," I say, changing the subject. "It looks lovely."

"It's my pleasure, darling," she replies, taking a slice of beef and putting it on her plate. "Now, Graham, did you get this beef from the butchers like I asked you to?"

"Yes, Mary. You said, 'Whatever you do, don't get the beef from a supermarket'. So I didn't."

"What's up with the beef from the supermarket, Dad?" I ask.

"Rob, if there's one thing I've learned over the years regarding your mother, it's don't question, just do." I turn my attention to Mum.

"What's wrong with the beef at the supermarket, Mum?"

"Well, you know people still haven't been vaccinated?" I nod, intrigued. "Well, they've started putting the vaccination in supermarket meat. And the last thing I want is to be double-jabbed or worse, triple-jabbed. But don't tell anyone, Rob. I've been sworn to secrecy," she finishes.

"And where the hell have you heard that, I say," laughing at the ridiculousness of the conversation.

"Margaret told me at the hairdresser on Tuesday."

"Mary!" my dad says in between mouthfuls, "I've told you, you need to change hairdressers. Every time you go there, you come home with a story more unbelievable than the last."

"Ok, we will change the subject then," she snaps.

"How's work, Rob?" I tell them all about the new role I've been given.

"Does it start straightaway?" my dad asks.

"No, it doesn't start till June, so I've got plenty of time to prepare for it," I reply.

"And do you know who you are going to be working with?" Mum asks.

"There are four of us altogether. There are two blokes, Andy and Paul, who I know are really good mates outside of work. The other person is a woman called Tiffany, who is the manager of the Rome branch. She's coming over until it's done. I've been told she's really good." "Well, we are proud of you, son," my mum says adoringly.

I help clear the plates and wash up while Mum sorts the pudding out. Dad sits in front of the TV, watching Formula One. After pudding, we sit for a bit. I notice my dad starting to get tired, so I figure it's time for me to leave. I put my coat on and wrap my scarf around my neck. Mum comes through with the leftover chili she promised me.

"Before you go," she begins. "Don't forget it's your brother's birthday next Thursday. Now, I know how you feel about him. And I'm not asking you to make a big song and dance about it. But if you could just text him a happy birthday, it would make me happy. So do it for me, please."

I tell her I will. She gives me a kiss on the cheek. Saying bye to my dad, I make my way back to the tube. I put the audiobook back on, but I'm too distracted to concentrate. All I can think about is my brother.

4. Brother Where Art Thou

Thursday 15th February 2024

I'm sitting at my desk contemplating what to have for dinner. When a text comes through from mum.

"Rob, don't forget it's your brother's birthday today. All I'm asking for is a simple happy birthday text. Love mum xxx"

She then sends me another message with his number which means I can't use the excuse that I didn't have it. I type the number out into my phone. *It's only a message, that's it, nothing has to come of it.* I sit there for 5 minutes and I'm yet to type anything. It shouldn't be this hard to send a birthday message, but when it's your brother, whom you haven't spoken to in 10 years, it is.
****

I'm three years older than my brother Jason. To say we aren't very close would be an understatement. He's always had my mum wrapped around his little finger. Whatever I had, Jason wanted, and whatever Jason wanted, he got. I remember when I was 14, I saw a keyboard in the music shop window. It was £200. I asked Mum if I could have it, and she told me that it was a lot of money and we couldn't afford it at that moment. But if I wanted it, I would have to get a paper round or wait until Christmas. So, I got myself a paper round that paid £12 a week. Every morning, I got up early and delivered papers before school. Every Saturday, I went to the music shop to look at it. It took me 17 weeks to be able to afford this keyboard. When I finally had enough money, me and dad went to fetch it. The bloke at the music shop was brilliant. He saw how excited I was and threw in a stand and a song and lyrics book to help get me started. I couldn't wait to get it home. I played that keyboard all weekend until my fingers ached. By the end of the weekend, I'd learned half of David Gray's This Year's Love.

The following Monday, I remember school feeling like it dragged on. I just couldn't wait to get back on it. When I finally got home, I chucked my bag down and raced upstairs. As I got to the top of the stairs, I could hear what sounded like someone trying to play a guitar with a spoon. As I passed Jason's bedroom, there he was, sitting on the bed with a shiny new guitar.
"Where did you get that from," I asked gobsmacked.
"Mum got it for me. She picked it up for me today. Do you like it?" he said, with the biggest shit-eating grin on his face.
I was always a docile kid. I never really back-chatted my parents or gave them too much grief. But this, I couldn't let go. I marched downstairs. Mum was in the living room doing some ironing.
"How come Jason's got a new guitar?" I asked, struggling to contain my anger.
"It's an early Christmas present," she replied, not even looking at me.
"Early Christmas present?" I snapped. "It's April. And anyway, I was told that I had to wait for Christmas or get a job in order to get that keyboard."
"I know, Rob, but you know what your brother's like. He wouldn't stop pestering me until I gave in,"
"Well, maybe that's what I should have done then," I said, spitefully. Even though we both know I wouldn't have done it.
"Anyway, you've got a keyboard, he's got a guitar. Now you can both play together," she said hopefully.
"Sorry Mum, but it's not going to happen." I made my way back upstairs. I could hear Jason still playing clumsily as I passed his room. Our eyes met, and he just smiled at me, victorious. I went to my bedroom and slammed the door behind me. That was just the start of a very strained relationship. The worst was yet to come.

When he turned 15, he fell in with the wrong crowd. Well, in fairness, he didn't fall in. He walked in with his arms open. He'd always been a show-off to anyone who would give him the time of day. So it was no surprise when he started knocking around with lads two years older than him, and it wasn't long before they were putting his skills to the test and getting him to nick stuff for them. He seemed to be quite good at it. Until he got caught, and Mum nearly died of embarrassment when the police brought him home. I remember Dad laying into him when he got home. But it did no good; he just shrugged his shoulders. He had no remorse for anything he did, no regret. Thankfully, I wasn't around to see much of it. By that point, I was just about to finish college and head off to Cambridge, and I spent most of my nights at Michelle's. But once again, where Jason was concerned, things were about to get even worse.

It was one of the rare days that I was home. I'd come to visit Mum to see how she was, and I remember taking my coat off and putting it on the rack at the bottom of the stairs. We chatted about general life, studies, and films we'd both seen. She knew better than to talk to me about Jason because she knew we didn't get along. I knew he was home because I could hear music coming from his bedroom. I shouted goodbye to Mum, who was in the kitchen, and took my coat off the rack. Jason came out of his bedroom and down the stairs. I nodded my head to acknowledge I'd seen him, and he nodded back. He looked a mess, all pale and clammy, like he hadn't slept in weeks. When he got to the bottom step, he lost his footing slightly. A small bag of white powder fell out of his pocket. I'm no expert on drugs, but I know what cocaine looks like. He tried to pick it up before I'd seen but it was too late. He looked at me panicking. "It's not mine, it belongs to a mate of mine. I'm looking after it for him." He protested. I looked at him. I didn't believe him and he knew I didn't but I never said anything. I just walked out and we never mentioned it again.

The week before I was due to go to university, Michelle and I started planning what weekends she would come up to see me. And what weekends I would come to see her. As the week wore on, I started to feel more emotional about leaving her. We'd been inseparable ever since we first got together and I was going to miss her a lot. We made the most of just being together. We went out for meals and tried to do some of the new things London had to offer that probably wouldn't be there the next time I came back.

On the last night, Mum and Dad wanted to treat me to a meal, just the four of us. But much to my delight, Jason didn't want to come. I offered to drive because I wanted a clear head for the next day. When I made the drive up to Cambridge. We found a nice Italian place and over-ordered everything from pizza to pasta. Mum and Dad shared a couple of bottles of wine and then proceeded to tell me how proud they were of me. Once we got home, it was late so Mum and Dad went up to bed. I stayed downstairs for a bit and watched some TV. I started drifting, so I decided to call it a night. As I walked past Jason's bedroom, I spotted one of my T-shirts. A T-shirt I'd been looking for. It must have been put in with his stuff accidentally. I went in to get it, and that's when I saw it. The silver glinting handle of a knife poking out from under the bed. I picked it up. I was so taken aback that I didn't hear the door open or Jason climbing the stairs. He entered the room.

"WHAT ARE YOU DOING IN HERE!" he shouted.
"What am I doing?" I said, trying not to wake Mum and Dad up. "Why do you have this?"
"That's none of your fucking business," he snapped.
"That's fine if you don't want to tell me. I'll just tell Mum and Dad," I answered back.
He took the knife off me and grabbed me by my shirt pushing me up against the door. With his forearm resting on my throat, the knife was inches away from my face. "You tell Mum and Dad and

it's the last thing you will ever do." He snarled, saliva flying from his mouth.

"Ok, ok," I replied. "I won't. Please, Jason, let me go." I said, tears streaming down my face. He pushed me out into the hallway and slammed his bedroom door. I went to my room and closed the door. I was shaking. I decided I had to get out of there that night. After a minute of silence, I heard his bedroom door open. I could feel my heart racing. I'd never been so afraid. But instead of coming towards me, I heard him go downstairs and out the front door. This was my chance to get out. I took out a pen and a piece of paper from my desk and began to write.

To Mum and Dad.
I've gone to Michelle's. I wanted to get an early start so I'm driving to Cambridge first thing. Thank for you taking me out and for everything you've done for me.
Love Rob x

I placed the note on my desk and left the house. When I got to Michelle's, I was still shaking. She made me a cup of tea, and I told her what had happened. After a while, we went to bed. The next morning, we drove to Cambridge to get away from it all.

For the first week, I didn't sleep very much at all. Every time I tried to close my eyes, I was back in Jason's bedroom, pinned up against the door. But if time is the greatest healer, then distance must be a close second. Because knowing I was 53 miles away from him, made me feel safe. And because of that, I gradually put it to the back of my mind. This is a good job really, as I was about to spend the next three years doing a bachelor's degree in marketing. When I wasn't in class, I was either talking to Michelle on the phone or driving to see her. It was hard for the first six months because she lived in the same area as my parents, so I had to avoid bumping into Jason. But then they moved to Essex, so things got a lot easier.

The first weekend that my parents came up to visit me, I waited until I got Dad on his own and told him all about the night before I left. I'd never seen him so angry. He told me he would get rid of the knife and that it was probably best not to tell Mum. It's not as if he wanted to keep a secret from her. But when it came to Jason, she wore rose-tinted glasses, and he knew this would shatter her. I said that was fine, but I didn't want Jason visiting me. The second time my parents came to visit, I asked my dad how things were, and he told me that he'd wrapped the knife up in a carrier bag and threw it in the Thames. He told me that he sat my brother down and told him that if he ever did anything like that again he would tell Mum everything and he would be out. I'm not saying it worked but the next few visits Dad seemed a lot less stressed and Jason hadn't given them any more trouble which was all I cared about, so we never talked about it.

Over the next 3 years, things couldn't have gone better. I was flying at Cambridge and my relationship with Michelle was the best it had been; we talked on the phone all the time and I visited whenever I could. She helped her mum and dad run their family Greasy Spoon Café, which was getting rave reviews. It was labelled one of London's finest establishments. We even talked about getting a place together once I graduated.

Graduation morning came around, and I couldn't believe how fast the time had gone. I'd passed with a 2.1 in Marketing. All the weight of the last 3 years was off my shoulders. I was living the rock and roll lifestyle of celebrating with a cup of tea and a slice of toast when the phone rang; it was Mum. "Hi, darling," she said excitedly, "Happy graduation day! We can't wait to see you, even Jason's coming." It was like someone had opened a window in the middle of December; the air around me went cold.
"Tell him he doesn't have to," I said nervously.

"Don't be silly, I've told him it's your big day and he needs to be here for it so we can celebrate as a family," she replied. "Anyway, I will let you go and get yourself ready. Love you, darling. Bye Bye."
"Bye, Mum," I replied and hung up. I paced up and down. I was scared. I hadn't seen him in 3 years. *Shit, this was bad. It's okay*, I told myself. Mum, Dad, and Michelle were going to be there. He wouldn't say or do anything in front of them. I needed to forget about it and just enjoy the day. I had to be at the university 90 minutes before the ceremony. So, I put my robe on and made my way.
When we arrived at the senate house, I tried to take my mind off Jason. But as I chatted with fellow students and teachers, all I could think about was his arm on my throat and the knife held to my face. Mum texted me, telling me they'd arrived. I went to the car park to meet them. I watched as Mum, Dad, and Michelle got out and breathed a sigh of relief when I didn't see Jason. "I thought Jason was coming?" I said, trying not to sound too excited.
"He is, he's coming on the train," Mum replied, bringing me crashing back down to earth. When it was time, I put on my BA gown and hood. Jason still hadn't turned up. Every second he wasn't there, I felt less nervous. My big moment arrived. My name was called, and it was my turn to kneel before the vice chancellor and offer my hand. I stood, bowed, and was given my certificate. I scanned the crowd for Mum, Dad, and Michelle. I spotted Michelle immediately, her camera pointing at me, telling me to smile. Then I saw Mum at the back of the house crying. But it wasn't until I saw Dad's arm around her shoulders that I realized they weren't tears of joy. I made my way over to them. "Mum, are you okay?" I asked, worried.
Dad answered for her. "Rob, I'm sorry, but we have to go. It's your brother; he's in the hospital. drug overdose."
After that, I didn't feel much like celebrating, so Michelle and I packed up my stuff, and I left Cambridge early. I stayed with Michelle at her parents' house for a few months. During that time,

Jason woke up and went home to be kept under watch. Mum asked me to come and see him, but I told her I never wanted to see him again. He had ruined what was supposed to be one of the best days of my life. After that, I got a job at Amato's, and Michelle and I started renting the house. The only time I saw Mum and Dad was when they came to visit. It wasn't until my brother moved out and they downsized, that I knew it was safe to go and visit them.

****

I'm still staring at the blank screen. Maybe it is time to bury the hatchet after all 10 years is a long time. I type out a simple message.

Hey Jason, it's Rob (your brother) happy birthday.

I wasn't expecting a reply, but just after 20 minutes, I get a text back, even more simpler than mine.

Thanks bro. It reads and I leave it at that.

5. Breakfast with Tiffany

4 months later

Monday, the 17th of June 2024

When a relationship ends, it's like being lost in a forest without a map or compass. You have no idea if you are going in the right direction or not. But what you do know is that if you don't keep moving, you could be stuck there forever.
By the time June comes around, I've settled into a routine and I'm adapting to single life the best way I can. I'm a lot more adventurous with cooking – then again, anything was more adventurous than the ready-made meals I'd been eating when Michelle left.
Speaking of Michelle, I've still not heard a single thing from her. I left her another voicemail basically saying that I miss her and that if she goes scuba diving on her travels, I hope she gets bitten by a sea turtle. When that's once again unanswered, I decide that enough is enough. I have to dust myself off and get on with life. Especially, with the excitement and preparation of Amato's new project growing day by day. I still miss Michelle, and I'm not fully over her, but I have to admit that as time goes by, it is getting easier and there are days I hardly even think about her.
By far, the best thing to come out of her leaving is the amount of time I get to spend with Dad. I accompany him to record fairs. I watch his kid in a toy shop enthusiasm, as he hunts for rare vinyls and bargains. I've also joined his golf club. We play most Sundays, and I must say I'm getting quite good. Not Rory McIlroy good, but good enough to hold my own against Dad.
A lot of men will say that their dads are their best friends, but for me, he's probably my only friend. I never really clicked with the lads at Cambridge. While they were out drinking their body weight in tequila, I was in my dorm room drinking red wine, reading

Jonathan Tropper, and watching Game of Thrones. I mean, there was the odd occasion when Michelle and I would go out for a meal with one of her friends and her latest fella, but it never went any further than that.

A few weeks ago, I received an email from my boss, and this is how it read:

Hey Rob, exciting news! We've got a start date for the new project. It will be Monday, the 17th of June. Now, I know you normally come in at 9:00 am, but I would like you to come in at 8:00 am just for that day. We are having a "Meet the Team" breakfast in the conference room so we can all have a chat and get to know each other a little bit before we really get into the swing of things. I hope you're as excited as I am. I think this could really take our company to the next level.

Steve Smith.

I go out and buy myself some new suits, some ties, and a pair of oil-black shoes. I really want to look the part and go in feeling fresh, so the night before, I make sure I have an early night. The next morning, I get up early, shower, and have a shave. I put on a charcoal grey suit with a navy blue tie and spray my neck with a dash of Amato's. As a sort of rule, everyone in the office wears Amato aftershave. At the end of the day, you are representing the company, and wearing a rival aftershave would be like turning up to work at Tesco wearing a Sainsbury's uniform. As I'm having breakfast at work, which is something I've never done before, I just make myself a cup of tea. I'm starting to get nervous; I can feel it in the pit of my stomach. I take a deep breath, finish my tea, and pick up my briefcase before leaving the house.

I get to the tube stop, and the sign says 4 minutes until the next one. I take my headphones out of my inside pocket and slip them on. I need something calming, so I put on Fleet Foxes. I let the soft melodic folk music wash over me while I brace myself for the unknown.

I get to the office, and Clive lets me into the building. I walk up the stairs and enter the main area. It's a Monday morning, but it feels different. The whole place seems anxious but excited in anticipation of what could be. I make my way to the long wide conference room with its many chairs and big projector screen. I've only ever been in here twice. Once, I had to listen to an ex-firefighter talk about fire safety. Interestingly, he was a smoker. That's like the chairperson of an AA meeting talking about the dangerous effects of alcohol with a can of beer in their hand. The second time was when someone in the office claimed that someone had taken their packed lunch, and we all had to go into the conference room one by one to find out who the culprit was.

Andy and Paul are already inside, tucking into breakfast, and the smell hits me as soon as I open the big glass doors. There are sausages, eggs, bacon, and hash browns. Cereal, toast, bagels, and croissants. Tea, coffee, espressos, and lattes. Amato's has gone all out, and it smells amazing. Steve isn't around, so I help myself to a small plate of one of everything and make myself a cup of tea.

Amato's isn't one of those places where everyone stands around the water coolers swapping stories, so I don't know a great deal about Andy and Paul. I make my way over to introduce myself properly. Andy is dark-skinned and very slender. The type of physique you get from years of playing sport. His chin is purposely stubbled. He shakes my hand and introduces himself as a poor man's Idris Elba.

Paul is the complete opposite; he's lanky and milky white. He looks like he could get heatstroke standing too close to a radiator. We start chatting, and I learn that they are just as nervous as I am, which puts me at ease. The glass doors open, and Steve enters. He sees that I've arrived.

"Ah, Rob, you're here," he says, relieved. "So we are just waiting on Tiffany."

You know those cheesy American romcoms where the female protagonist is first introduced to the story, the elevator dings and she walks down the corridor like a shampoo advert, hair bouncing around in slow motion, and everyone stares open-mouthed? Well, when she walks through the door, it's not quite like that, but all three of us can see how attractive she is. I don't mean in an objectifying, group of builders, in hi-vis jackets, wolf-whistling kind of way, but an honest appreciation that another human being is attractive.

"Hi, I'm Tiffany," she says, smiling.

And now we really are in trouble because it's an open-mouthed smile showing off a set of perfectly straight, pearly white teeth. She's wearing a pair of formal black trousers, a white blouse, and a black jacket. She's about 5ft 3in with shoulder-length dyed blonde hair, and wearing a pair of black glasses.

When it's my turn to introduce myself, I shake her hand, hoping mine isn't sweaty. As I do, I get a slight hint of her perfume before noticing that she's wearing a wedding ring, and my heart sinks a little. She helps herself to a croissant and a mug of green tea. When everyone's done eating, Steve tells us all to take a seat.

"Thank you all for coming and congratulations for getting to this stage," he begins, like it's an episode of The Chase, and all four of us are through to the final round.

"Now, firstly, I want to stress that there is no immediate time frame on this. I've spoken with Luca Amato and the investors, and we want to give you guys time and space to get creative without feeling any pressure, so it takes as long as it takes. Now, I've spoken personally with Tiffany, and she is 100% committed to staying in London until it's done."

I get a little feeling of elation when he says this, even though she's married, and I probably wouldn't have any chance if she wasn't. Steve is still talking. "There is a lot to go through, such as:

- Name of the new aftershave

- Bottle shape

- Target audience

- Venue for the advert

- Music for the advert

- Actors/actresses for the advert

- Etc., etc.

"Oh, and one more thing, whatever plans you had for dinner tonight, cancel them. I've booked us a table. I want us to get to know each other on a more personal level outside the confines of this conference room. Think of it as a team bonding exercise. Thank you, and let's get started," he says excitedly.

We spend the afternoon brainstorming, looking at adverts from rival aftershave companies, and just adverts for other products in general. We decide that if we give the product a name first, then we can bounce ideas off that.
"How about Desire?" Paul says confidently.
"I'm not sure about that; desire is a dangerous emotion," Tiffany replies assertively.
"How do you mean?" Paul shoots back.
"Well, let me ask you this question: have you ever pretended to like a song, film, or a piece of art that another person likes in order to sleep with them?"
He thinks about it tentatively.
"Yeah, I would say I have."

"There you go, that's the power of desire. Just like a supermodel simply posting the word "bored" on a social media post is bound to get more likes than an average Joe posting a quote from Shakespeare. And it's all because her profile picture is her in a bikini, see what I'm saying? Desire is one of the most dangerous emotions; it clouds people's judgment."

"But sex sells!" Andy chips in.

"You are totally right, but what if we broke that mould."

"That is an interesting idea," Steve purrs, sounding more impressed than I've ever heard him.

The day flies by and we already have a few ideas in the pipeline. Steve decides to wrap it up for the day because it's gone 5 o'clock and he's starving.

The restaurant isn't far from the office, so we walk. It's a nice night. It's cloudy but warm. Leicester Square, as always, is heaving. If any of us thought we were going somewhere posh, then we were instantly disappointed. It's a bar and grill, but we're not paying, so that's a bonus. We're shown to our table, and Steve asks us all what we want to drink before going off to get them. An hour or so later, we are all on our fourth drink, and people are starting to shed their serious workplace skins and slip into their off-the-clock ones. That's the power of alcohol. It takes a group of 5 people, who before today knew very little about each other, to knowing each other's favourite bands, guilty pleasures, and what one thing they would save if their house were on fire. There's music playing, but not loud enough for us not to be able to talk. Paul is doing a brilliant job of subtly asking Tiffany questions without coming across as too nosy, and I'm hanging on to every word.

So far, I've found out she's 31, Her husband works in precision machinery, She loves animals and always wanted to be a vet, but couldn't imagine getting over the animals she couldn't save. One day, she wants to go on an African safari. "Right, my turn. We will start with relationships. Paul, what's your status?" she asks.

"I'm single, but not by choice. I can't seem to make them stay for more than 3 months," he admits, only half joking.

"What about you, Andy?"

"I'm single, but it's by choice. There's just something about the thrill of the chase that I love," he replies.

She turns to me.

"Rob, what's your story?"

"I'm also single, but only until recently. I was with my girlfriend for 12 years," I answer sheepishly.

"How old are you?" she asks, a little confused.

"I'm 28,"

"High school sweethearts," she says coyly,

"So what happened?"

"We wanted different things," I reply, turning away.

She doesn't poke any further, sensing my reluctance. There's a moment of silence before Paul breaks it. "I thought we were eating."

The music stops and a man in a cheap suit shouts into a microphone.

"LADIES AND GENTLEMEN, IT'S TIME FOR THE MOMENT YOU'VE ALL BEEN WAITING FOR!"

Even though most people like us have only been here for an hour.

"IT'S THE MONDAY NIGHT HOTDOG EATING CONTEST. TWO TEAMS WILL BATTLE IT OUT FOR A PLACE ON THE WALL OF FAME!"

He continues, pointing to a wall that none of us can see.

"SO WITHOUT ANY FURTHER ADO, LETS MEET THE TEAMS. TEAM 1: DAVES AUTOSHOP."

Four blokes get up and make their way to a long table with four chairs facing the front.

"AND THEIR CONTESTANTS, THE AFTERSHAVE COMPANY AMATO'S."

We all look at each other stunned.

"I did say it was a team bonding evening," Steve says, smiling.

"You are joking, are you? A team bonding exercise is rock climbing or an escape room, not a hotdog eating contest," Andy cries.

"I can't actually do it, I'm a vegetarian," Tiffany says, ruling her out.

"Us four, it is then," Steve says, completely unnerved.

"I'll do it," Paul volunteers, a lot more drunk than the rest of us.

"It's like the late great Ronan Keating once said, life is a roller coaster, you've just got to ride it."

I laugh.

"First of all, Ronan Keating is still very much alive, and secondly, that's a terrible reference."

"What about you, Rob?" Steve asks, looking at me.

I don't know if it's the drink, the occasion, or the fact that I don't want to seem boring in front of Tiffany, but I agree to do it. This must be what Tiffany was talking about earlier when she mentioned desire. So off we go. Me, Steve, and two blokes, who before today I'd only made small pleasantries with, make our way to face the competition.

"NOW THAT WE HAVE OUR TEAMS, LETS GO OVER TO THE RULES." Shouts the man in the suit, who I'm guessing is the manager.

"EACH CONTESTANT HAS 2 MINUTES AND 30 SECONDS TO EAT AS MANY HOTDOGS FOR THEIR TEAM BEFORE THE TIME RUNS OUT."

And it was as simple as that.

"THE TEAM TO GO FIRST IS DAVE'S AUTO SHOP, CONTESTANT 1, ARE YOU READY?"

The man in the first seat, who could quite easily be Dave, nods and a plate of 10 hotdogs is put in front of him. The timer starts, and he wolfs down the first one with ease and I think we could be in trouble. In the end, he manages five.

The man in the second chair has a go, and he also manages five. It's contestant three's turn, and he manages six, and finally, the last contestant manages four. "WELL DONE, DAVE'S AUTOSHOP! YOU MANAGED TO EAT 20 HOTDOGS. LET'S SEE IF AMATO'S CAN BEAT THAT!" shouts the host, clearly in his element. We take our seats, and I realize I'm last, and if I wasn't nervous before, I am now. The thought then occurs to me that this is probably the reason no waiter/waitress ever came to our table. Andy goes first and manages to eat seven hotdogs. I'm impressed and relieved. Then it's Paul's turn. The klaxon for the timer sounds. Paul just sits there staring at the plate of hotdogs. He's so intoxicated that he probably sees 20 instead of 10. 20 seconds go by and he still hasn't picked one up. I can hear the crowd murmuring to themselves. As he fallen asleep? What is he doing, deciding which one looks the best? *Just pick one up, Paul!* I want to shout, but I don't.

Finally, he chooses a hotdog and starts eating. When the klaxon sounds to end his two-and-a-half minutes, he's managed to eat two hotdogs. *"Great,"* I think to myself, *"this is going to be all on me, isn't it?"* But I'm saved by the human dustbin that is Steve. He eats the hotdogs like his life depends on it. I don't even think he's chewing them; he's just shovelling them in. He manages to eat 9 hotdogs. Even the host can't believe what he's seen. I work it out to win, I only have to eat 3 hotdogs. I can do that. All of a sudden, I feel two hands on my shoulders. I turn around, and it's Paul.

"Come on, Rob. You've got this. Don't let us down," he says, like he's my trainer, psyching me up for a prize fight. This coming from the bloke who managed to eat two.

"LADIES AND GENTLEMEN, THIS IS IT, CONTESTANT FOUR. ARE YOU READY?"

I nod. Most people have lost interest; they are pretty confident I'm going to eat three, so they go about their night. The plate of hotdogs is put in front of me, and the timer starts. I pick the first one up and take a big bite. The bun is stale, and the sausage could use another 5 minutes. Then, I remember I'm not here to review them; I'm here to eat them. I finish the first one.

I manage to get three down with 10 seconds to spare, so I just let the timer run out. We've won, but it's not very dramatic, much to the disappointment of the host and the remaining people watching. We get our picture taken for the wall and return to our seats. Steve calls it a night and tells us not to stay out too long,

Andy tries his luck with a woman at the bar,

Paul is still reeling from our victory. "How about another drink for the man of the hour?" He says.

It was two and a half minutes and, technically, all I did was have my dinner, but I say yes and he heads to the bar, leaving me and Tiffany alone for the first time.

"Can I ask you a question? I say.

"Yes of course," She replies.

"Are you really a vegetarian?"

She looks at me bashfully.

"No, but it got me out of it, didn't it"

"Very smart," I say, impressed.

Just then, a man taps Tiffany on the shoulder, and her look tells me she doesn't know him.

"Can I help you?" she asks, politely.

"Can I buy you a drink?" Clearly, he has had a few too many himself.

"Sorry, I'm married," she says, holding up the hand with her wedding ring on.

"Is this your husband then?" the man says, not finished with the conversation.

"Not like it's any of your business, but no." I can see she's getting annoyed.

"Well, is your husband here?" He's refusing to be rejected.

"No, he isn't, but again, that's none of your business."

She gets louder and more annoyed.

"Why won't you have a drink with me then? Afraid you'll get tempted?"

He winks at her, the wink has no subtlety to it, it's almost in slow motion. Tiffany looks at him and starts counting on her hands.

- Jump naked into a nettle bush.
- Let Edward Scissorhands give me a root canal.
- Shave my armpits with a potato peeler.

He looks at her confused.
"Sorry," She says not very apologetic.
"I was just naming things I'd rather do than go for a drink with you."
I laugh so hard, I think the man is going to swing for me, but instead, he stares at her for a minute.
"I don't have to take this. I'm a very important person with a very important job," he scolds.
"Oh yeah, what do you do?" Tiffany asks, intrigued.
"I work for a big media company. It's called Central Unit National Television," he replies, proudly.
I look across at Tiffany to see if she has worked out the abbreviation of the man's job the smile on her face tells me that she has. He turns and walks away.
"I think that's my cue to leave," she says, smiling. "Besides, I'd better ring Carlo." The use of her husband's name is like a dagger through the heart.
"See you tomorrow, Rob." She gets up and leaves.
Paul comes back with the drinks. Paul has the ability to pull conversations out of thin air; you never feel there's going to be an awkward silence with him. He's like a chameleon, adapting to whatever surroundings he's placed into, and I must admit it's oddly comforting. But after a few more drinks, he starts to get mopey.
We are talking about the aftershave and what it should be called.
"How about despair?" he says, sombrely.
"The slogan could be, 'It doesn't matter what you smell like, we are all going to die alone anyway.'"

"I think I'll call it a night," I say, standing up.

He downs his drink and comes with me.

"See you tomorrow," he says as he goes right and I go left.

When I get home, I climb into bed and relive one of the best nights I've had in a long time.

I love Michelle, and I'm always going to wonder where she is and what she's doing, and I'll never understand her decision to leave. But for the first time in 4 months, she isn't the woman I'm thinking about while going to bed. Why, oh why, does she have to be married?

6. Reservoir Frogs

Tuesday, the 18th of June 2024.

The next morning, I arrive at work and head to the conference room. Andy and Paul are already here.
"Do these two sleep here?" I think to myself as I enter.
They both appear a little worse for wear, each holding a hot mug of strong coffee.
"Morning," I say as I make myself a cup of tea and join them at the table.
"Last night was a blur," Paul groans between sips of coffee. "Rob, I apologize if I said anything inappropriate to you. I tend to act more immaturely the more pissed I become."
I smile at him. "Not at all. I thought you were funny."
"What about you, Andy? I saw you at the bar with that woman. Did anything happen?" Paul asks.
Andy takes a sip of his coffee. "Yeah, we ended up going back to her place, and I'll tell you what, she knew her way around the bedroom," he says smugly.
Paul laughs.
"What's funny?"
"Well, I hope she did. It's her bedroom. You'd be a bit freaked out if you went upstairs, got to the bedroom door, and she turned to you and said, 'You'll have to bear with me, this is my first time going in here as well.'"
The three of us laugh together.
It's so nice to have a genuine conversation with two guys that doesn't feel forced or awkward.
It makes me feel a pang of sadness that I've never had that with Jason. But I look forward to working with Paul and Andy, They are all right.
Steve joins us shortly after, and again we are waiting on Tiffany, but she does have the furthest to come. When she walks through

the door, she looks more attractive than she did yesterday, which I didn't think was possible, but she does.

I realize I need to snap out of this Tiffany trance, but every time she opens her mouth, I'm like a moth to a flame. I need her to say or do something ugly to put me off her, which sounds horrible, but I can't focus properly.

It's mid-afternoon, and we are discussing the name of the aftershave. "Has anyone got any ideas?" Steve says hopefully.

When nobody says anything, I take my opportunity.

"Well, I was thinking, when a bloke puts on a nice expensive aftershave, it doesn't just smell nice, it makes them feel more confident. We need a name that portrays confidence."

"What are you thinking?" Steve asks, intrigued.

"Well, firstly, and I don't mean to sound blunt, but at the moment, we are the low-cost option for men who wear aftershave for everyday use, such as working in offices, retail stores, and anything else that relates to working with the public. But when it comes to the more special occasions like weddings, nights out, job interviews, that sort of thing, they use their best aftershave. If we are going to rival the likes of Versace, Prada, and Paco Rabanne, we need a name and an advert that portrays confidence. We want men to buy it and think, 'This is the aftershave I want to get married in, or this is the aftershave that is going to get me that job'."

As I finish, I look around the table for a reaction. Steve looks impressed, but it's hard to be sure.

"I agree," Tiffany says, smiling.

"So we need a name that describes confidence then," Andy chips in.

"What about Dutch courage?" Paul replies.

"I'm not sure we can call an Italian aftershave Dutch courage," Steve says.

"What about liquid confidence?" Andy suggests.

"Sounds like a cocktail," Tiffany chimes.

She chews the end of her pen before speaking.

"What about poised?"

For a moment, no one says a word. We all just let it play out in our heads and still, no one disagrees.

"Poised for men," Steve says, testing it out on his tongue. "Yeah, I like that."

There's still so much to decide, but it feels like a breakthrough.

It's 4:30 pm when Steve decides that's enough for the day. As I'm getting my stuff together, I'm saying bye to Tiffany when Paul approaches us.

"Me and Andy are going for a curry, do you fancy it?"

"Are you talking to me or Tiffany?" I reply, taken aback.

"Both of you," he replies.

I think of how much of a laugh last night was, and how gutted I was when it ended. Plus, if Tiffany says yes, I get to spend more time with her, which isn't healthy but is all I can think about. Besides, what else am I going to do, go home, cook a meal for one, and watch old episodes of Friends?

"Yeah, sounds good to me," I reply finally.

"Tiffany?" Paul asks.

"Sorry, I can't, I'm afraid. I promised Carlo I'd FaceTime him."

My heart sinks a little.

I'm taken to a posh little Indian restaurant in Holborn. A waitress leads us downstairs. It's got booth seats all around the back wall, and tables of four scattered across the rest of the restaurant. The carpet is bright red, and there are frames of Indian culture plastered across the walls. It looks a bit romantic for three blokes having a bit of food, but Andy ensures me the food is amazing. We order three bottles of beer, and the waitress brings them over with a load of poppadoms and a selection of dips to nibble on while we decide what we want. When it's all ordered, the waitress leaves us to it.

"What do you two think of Tiffany then?" Andy asks, clearly wanting to get our opinion for a while but never got us both alone. Luckily, Paul jumps in feet first.

"I mean, she's gorgeous, smart, funny, and she's got great taste in music. What's not to like?" He pauses to dip a poppadom in yogurt and mint before continuing.

"But she's also married to an Italian machinist who's probably tall, built like a brick shithouse, and rescues cats from trees."

I realize I have to add something. "Paul's right, someone like that doesn't stay single for long." And it's enough to kill the conversation.

The food comes out, and it smells amazing. I've gone for a chicken bhuna, pilau rice, and a cheese naan, which falls apart in my hand as I pull it.

"So, Rob, what are you going to do once this new product puts us all on the map?" Paul mumbles, with a mouth full of food.

"What do you mean?"

"Well, I googled this investor, and this man has got money coming out of his ears. Steve talks about a new product to rival the big aftershave brands, a TV advert, actors, and actresses. I think he's talking big time. Proper famous people, not some amateur stage production of Oliver-type famous, and we will be the ones to be credited for putting it all together. Do you know what doors that could open up for us?"

This, what Paul is saying now has never occurred to me.

"I've actually never given it any thought. What about you guys?"

"I want to create my own game show," he replies.

"Here we go again," Andy sighs, rolling his eyes.

"Have I missed something?" I laugh. "He comes up with these ridiculous game show ideas that would never work."

"Ignore him, Rob. He's just jealous."

"Like what?" I ask, intrigued.

"Well, I'm working on one at the minute called Reservoir Frogs."

I realize he's serious.

"And what's that?"

"A load of frogs are let loose in a reservoir, and the contestants go around with nets. The winner is the one that catches the most."

Andy laughs, and I laugh, and then finally Paul does too.

When we've finished eating, we stay for a couple more drinks. We talk about music, TV shows, films, and books.

When we get to the subject of families, I tell them about Mum and Dad but don't mention Jason. I never expected to bond with Andy and Paul as much as I have over the past couple of days, and I don't think I've laughed this much in a long time either. I can see that they've been mates for a very long time, and I'm grateful that they include me in every conversation. So when it comes to talking about relationships, I tell them all about Michelle.

"Bloody hell, mate, that is rough," Andy says when I've finished, but it feels good to get it off my chest.

On the way home, I stop off at the bookshop and pick up "Birdsong" by Sebastian Faulks, and "High Fidelity" by Nick Hornby. I get home, have a shower, make myself a cup of tea, and I'm just about to pick up "Birdsong," When the phone rings and it's Mum.

"Hi, darling," she says, and it sounds like she's also had a couple of drinks. "How's work?"

I tell her it's going really well, but I don't mention the people I'm working with, especially not Tiffany.

"And how's your love life?" she asks, and now I know she's had a couple of drinks.

"It's non-existent, Mum. I've not really had the time," I lie, because I've just spent the evening with Andy and Paul, and now I'm sitting at home doing nothing.

"Well, you need to make time, Rob," she says sternly.

"You can't wait around forever for Michelle to come back because she might not, you know!"

And I do know. It's been 4 months, and chances are I will never see her again, especially with her not having any family here. Why would she come back to London?

"Let me set you up with someone," she says.

"No thanks, Mum."

"Yes, Rob, it will be good for you. My friend Margaret's got a daughter who's 30. She's single. I'll set it up."

I know there's no point in fighting it, so I don't say anything, and she moves on quickly. "That wasn't what I was ringing for. I want to know what you're doing for Christmas this year? I know we normally come to you, but you're on your own now, aren't you?" she keeps reminding me. "So, do you want to come to us?"

"Will Jason be there?" I ask.

"There's a very big chance he will be," she replies.

"Ok, I'll come," I say.

For a minute, I think she's hung up because she doesn't speak.

"Really?" she finally says.

"Yeah, why not? I think it's time we let bygones be bygones." And I actually mean it because this year seems to be the year of new beginnings. Newly single, new job role, new mates.

"Thank you so much, Rob. You don't know what this means to me," she says, like I've just told her she's won the lottery.

"Right, I better go tell your dad," she beams.

"Bye, darling," she finishes and ends the call. I pick up birdsong and begin to read. I just hope I haven't made a big mistake.

7. I've got a golden ticket

It's Saturday morning and I'm pushing a shopping trolley around a very crowded Supermarket. There are two things I hate about shopping. Number one: People who bump into people they know and stand chatting in the middle of the aisle, completely in the way. Number two: Retired people who have had all week to do their shopping, but decided to come at the weekend and take forever to choose a loaf of bread.

I'm down the meat aisle deciding whether to have either sausages or a pork chop, when I hear a song playing through the speakers, it's Get Lucky by Daft Punk and Pharrell Williams. You know when a song transports you back to a time? Well, that's what this song does to me.

****

April 2013.

It's the year 2013, HMV goes into administration, traces of horse meat are found in burgers, the phrases twerk and selfie are added to the dictionary, and everyone wishes they hadn't. I turn 18 in January, and Mum and Dad keep urging me to drive because they are fed up with taking me to college. I really don't want to, but they buy me lessons for my birthday, so I kind of have to. I won't lie, I hate it. There's something about a driving instructor; they are the nicest people in the world when they pick you up, but as soon as they swap seats and sit in the passenger seat, they become the headmistress from Matilda.

They explain the basics, tell you to start the car, you take the wheel and drive around for 5 minutes. They say things like, "good", "yeah, that's it!", "well done", but as soon as you stall the car, they shout at you like you've driven into a wall. I hated it. Every week when I knew I had a lesson, I would look at the clock and the closer it got to the time, the more I panicked. If they were 5 minutes late, I used to get excited and think they'd forgotten. Then I'd hear the car, see the driver, and panic all over again. The number of times I wanted to quit was unbelievable, but Dad said that if I passed my test by August, he would buy me a car, a second-hand one, but still, it was a car. So, I knuckled down and by mid-July, I was deemed ready for my test.

I took my seat in the waiting room and a bloke who looked old enough to remember the first ever car called my name. I followed him out into the car park. I got in fastened my seatbelt put it into gear and tried to set off with the handbrake on stalling the car.

"I've failed haven't," I said, getting ready to get out of the car.

"I can't technically fail you if we've not actually moved yet," he replied.

"Start again take your time and you'll be fine." So I took a breath and started again and somehow I passed. It was one of the Greatest feelings I'd ever experienced. I couldn't wait to tell Mum, Dad, and Michelle. Dad stuck to his promise and got me a second-hand Nissan Micra. My brother, the car enthusiast, laughed and said it was a bag of shit. But to me, it was four wheels. I'd never been into cars and as long as it had a CD player, (which it did) I was golden.

Two weeks later it was Michelle's 18th birthday, and I wanted to make her a birthday gift. We had been going out for nearly two years, and she told me the only birthday gift she wanted was to lose her virginity. I was so relieved when she added, "To you Rob."

She told me she wanted to do it after her party, which she was having at her house.

When you tell an 18-year-old lad that you want to have sex with him, that is pretty much all he thinks about until it happens. So, in my aroused teenage state, I made her a mixed CD, and the first song on the CD was "Get Lucky" by Daft Punk. I also managed to record a birthday message over the top of it, one minute into the song. It went something like this:

"Hey Michelle, it's your boyfriend Rob (in case she didn't know it was me). Happy 18th Birthday! I've made you a CD of some of your favourite songs, starting with 'Get Lucky' by Daft Punk, and hopefully, I'll get very lucky tonight."

When you turn 18, you start to believe you're this fully grown adult and that your ideas can't be stupid because you're not a kid anymore.

I wrapped up the gift and walked it to her house on the morning of her birthday.

She only lived around the corner, so there was no point in taking the car. She took me upstairs, and I gave her the CD. She opened it there and then and placed it into the CD player.

"Don't listen to it yet," I said. "We will listen to it later," I added with a wink.

Later that afternoon, I got a phone call from my mum, telling me she needed me to come home. She had made a load of food for me to take to the party because you should never go to a party empty-handed.

"Bloody hell, Mum," I said, when I saw how much food she'd made. "It's not a massive party; it's only Michelle, her Mum and Dad, her 80-year-old nan, and 5 of her mates from school that she'd kept in touch with."

There was no way I could carry all this food.

I was going to have to drive back around.

Mum helped me load it into the car. I drove around the corner to Michelle's. By 8 o'clock, the party was in full flow, and since we were now 18, no one could technically stop us from drinking. But I was on a promise. So after the first two beers, I paced myself and carried my third beer around with me like a rare gem.

At about 10 o'clock, I could feel my phone vibrating in my pocket. It was Mum. I nipped outside to take it. "Hi, Mum, what's up?" I asked, trying to hide the disdain in my voice.

"I need you to pick your brother up. Me and your dad can't. We've both had a drink!"

"Well I can't either Mum. I've been drinking as well!"

"Okay, well you better not drive that car home Rob," she snapped frustrated.

"How stupid do you think I am? And anyway, I'm staying at Michelle's. I've got to go. I'm at a party. Bye."

I put my phone away and went back into the house. Michelle came dancing over. "You alright?" she asked, swaying her hips to the beat.

"Dance with me!" she whispered, giddy from a couple of glasses of Prosecco.

I moved my hips slightly, and as Michelle watched me attempt to dance, I noticed she was mouthing the words to Daft Punk's "Get Lucky." That's when I saw her CD player on the table. All the colour drained from my face.

"Why is your CD player down here?" I panicked. "The CD got jammed in the one downstairs, so I went to get mine," she replied, still dancing.

"Michelle, turn it off!" I stammered, but she didn't hear me. "MICHELLE, TURN IT OFF!" I shouted, but it was too late.

"Hey, Michelle, it's your boyfriend Rob. Happy 18th birthday. I've made you a CD of some of your favourite songs starting with 'Get Lucky' by Daft Punk, and hopefully, I'll get very lucky tonight."

I didn't wait for the reaction because I was out the door faster than a politician changing his mind.

It was midnight. I was lying in bed, and I hadn't heard from Michelle. I started to worry that this could be it between us. If she hadn't realized I was a complete moron by now, her mum and dad would be making sure she did. My phone lit up. It was a text message from Michelle.

"You still haven't given me the birthday present I asked for. Meet me outside mine, and for god's sake Rob, bring protection."

I was so excited that I nearly got out of bed like Charlie Bucket's Grandad does in Charlie and the Chocolate Factory. Dancing around and singing, "I've got a golden ticket." I walked to Michelle's, giving myself a pep talk on the way.

I got to Michelle's. She saw me from her bedroom window and she sneaked out.

We came away from the house so no one could hear us. It was then that we both realized that we had no idea where we were going to do it.

We couldn't do it at hers and we couldn't do it at mine either.

"We are going to have to do it in your car," she whispered.

"Ok," I whispered back, because at this point she could have suggested doing it in a thorn bush, and I'd of been up for it.

"Don't start the car though, because you'll wake Mum and Dad up. We need to push the car round the corner out of the way," she whispered frantically.

"Ok, I'll get in the car and you push it," I said, keeping my voice as low as I could.

"I can't push it, I'm not strong enough."

"Ok, I'll push the car and you steer it round the corner."

She climbed in and took the handbrake off.

I started to push the car towards the end of the street, which led to some garages, which was right. There was no left turn. As I pushed, she pressed the brakes.

I stopped and walked up the side of the car to the window. She wound it down. "What's the matter?" I asked, confused.

"When I get to the end, do I turn the steering wheel left or right?" she asked.

"Are you serious? There is no left turn, so you turn it right."

"I've never been behind the wheel of a car before. I didn't know if it was the opposite. Like left is right and right is left."

"How confusing would that be for a driver if it was the opposite?" I said, half annoyed, half laughing.

"Ok," she said, and I went back to pushing the car.

I don't know how, but we managed to get it into the garages and parked up. We both climbed into the back. She leaned over and started kissing me. "Have you brought protection?" she asked hopefully.

"Yeah, I've got a box of 12," I replied.

"TWELVE!' she shouted. "How many times do you think we are going to do it Rob?"

"Well what if I brought one and I lost it on the way, or ripped it getting out of the packet?"

"Then you should have just bought three."

"But what if mum found the box, saw that there were three missing and thought I was some sort of sex-crazed lunatic?"

"Just put it on, will you," she said, impatiently.

"Just put it on, will you," I **repeated**. "That's not very romantic!"

"Rob, we are in the back of your Nissan Micra and it smells like a rugby team's changing room. I think we are past the point of romance."

What followed was the best 1 minute and 45 seconds of my life so far.

8. Volunteer Work

Friday 5th of July.

It's a few weeks later, and we are in the conference room. Steve isn't in today; he's busy with meetings. We take advantage by wearing casual clothes. It's a good thing that we are because it's 23°C and far too hot for a shirt and tie. Tiffany is wearing a pair of blue jeans and a white Blondie t-shirt. It's the first time I've seen her outside of her work clothes, and she looks gorgeous. Her jeans hug her slender figure, and I can't help but steal glances. In the last couple of weeks, we have managed to come up with a design for the bottle. We've gone for heavy and grandiose. We want it to sit proudly on people's dressing tables. We are currently working on what sort of music genre would work best for a TV advert: slow and soft, or fast, heavy, and suspenseful, that kind of thing. We put down the pens and take a break.
"What's your top 3 books of all time?" Tiffany asks everyone, breaking what was a painfully long silence.
"I'll go first," Andy says, who I didn't even know was a reader. "3. Invincible."
"Ooh, is that like a tense thriller, where the detectives are chasing a serial killer who thinks he's invincible?" Tiffany asks, intrigued.
"Not quite," Andy replies, laughing.
"So what is it then?"
"It's the story of Arsenal's unbeaten season."
So, I was right: he isn't much of a reader. He starts again.
"3: Invincible, 2: Ian Wright's autobiography (Arsenal player), 1: The Mechanic, the Secret World of the F1 Pitlane."
Paul goes next.
"3: Submarine by Joe Dunthorne, 2: The Secret Diary of Adrian Mole by Sue Townsend, 1: The Hitchhiker's Guide to the Galaxy by Adam Douglas."
Clearly Paul likes a good laugh.

"Your turn, Rob," she says, turning to me.

I think for a moment.

"Ok, number 3 is Norwegian Wood by Haruki Murakami. Number 2 is Atonement by Ian McEwan, and number 1 is One Day by David Nicholls."

"Bloody hell," she says when I finish.

"What? Don't you like those books?"

"Yeah, I love them. But you've chosen three heartbreakingly gut-wrenching love stories."

I think about it, and she's right – all three books are tragic romances. No wonder my own life has followed suit.

My girlfriend of 12 years has left me, and I'm falling in love with a woman I can't have.

I imagine Morgan Freeman narrating the film adaptation of my story. "Rob saw no other option than to move to the harbour and become a lighthouse keeper, to get away from the agony that was his life," he would say as the credits rolled.

"Come on then, what's yours, Tiffany?" Paul says.

"Number 3: The Bell Jar. Number 2: The Great Gatsby, and number 1, without a doubt, has got to be Invincible: The Story of Arsenal's Unbeaten Season."

Andy's head whips around so fast I think he's broken his neck. I nearly spit my tea out. Paul laughs, and then Andy does too.

"I'm joking. Number 1 is To Kill a Mockingbird by Harper Lee."

For some women, the prospect of working this closely with three single men, I imagine it to be very intimidating. But you can see her confidence has gotten her to where she is. She leads most of the discussions, knows when to have a laugh, and when to be serious. And Most of the innovative ideas have been hers. She listens, she asks questions, but she doesn't pry. She's confident but doesn't brag. And she has this rare ability to make you feel good about yourself. The more time I spend with her, the more I fall for her. I sometimes wish she would come out with us after work, which has become a regular thing for me. Paul and Andy often ask her, but she's always going back to her hotel to FaceTime her husband, which I understand because if I was still with Michelle and I had to go work in another country, I would be doing the exact same thing. I know it's selfish of me, but I just really like her company.

"Right, let's do films next. They don't have to be in any particular order this time. Andy?" she says excitedly.

"Fast and the Furious, Lock Stock and Two Smoking Barrels, Casino Royale,"

He rattles off quickly.

"Paul?"

"Anchorman, Inception, One Flew Over the Cuckoo's Nest," he says after a few minutes.

"Rob?"

I'd been thinking about mine while it was Paul and Andy's turn.

"Dead Poets Society, Memento, Lord of the Rings: The Two Towers," I reply.

Tiffany doesn't say anything.

"Tiffany? Aren't you going to say yours?" Paul says after a while.

"They're really soppy, aren't they? I bet they're Titanic and The Notebook," Andy teases.

"No, there's just no point in saying mine. Two of them are the same as Rob's. I would swap Memento for Kill Bill, but the other two are the same," she replies, deflated.

I feel elated and pathetic at the same time. I'm like a kid at school who's just found out the girl he likes has got the same lunchbox as him.

I get home around 5:00 pm, and I do a bit of housework. When I finish, I realize I've got a missed call from Mum, so I ring her back.

"Hi, Mum, is everything alright?" I ask, hoping that it is.

"Yeah, everything's fine," she replies. "Just ringing to see if you're nervous about your date?"

"What date?" I ask, confused.

"Your date with Margaret's daughter is tonight at 7:00 pm. I told you about it the other day."

"No you didn't Mum," I say and we both know she didn't. "I'm not going, Mum."

"She's meeting you outside Tottenham Court Road Tube Station, she's picked the restaurant, and she's got herself all dolled up. You can't stand her up Rob. Do you know what that can do to a person?" she says, really laying it on thick.

"Sorry, Mum, but I'm not ready and I don't feel like it. I'll speak to you soon. I've got to go. Bye," I hang up the phone.

I carry on with the housework, but the guilt eats away at me, which is ridiculous because I don't even know the woman. I don't even know her name or what she looks like, and yet I'm picturing her waiting for me outside a tube station, checking her watch and wondering when to call it. I look at the clock; it's 6:00 pm.

"Fine, I'll go," I say to no one.

I have a shower and a shave before drying myself in front of the full-length mirror that is attached to one of the wardrobes. I look at myself naked. A design flaw that all humans have is that they can look at themselves naked and pick out at least one thing they don't like about themselves or something they wish was better. For me, I'm skinny everywhere, apart from a small rotund little beer belly. I also wish my nose was smaller, and because I've got jet black hair, you can see the grey hairs shining through, even at the young age of 28. It's like I've brushed my hair with emulsion. The only saving grace that we all have, is that nobody is perfect. Because if you think you're perfect, then you're arrogant, and arrogance is the ugliest flaw anyone could ever own. I spray myself with Ted Baker aftershave, put on a khaki green shirt, and some black jeans and make my way to the tube station. 6:30 pm, plenty of time. I start to feel a bit nervous because deep down I'm hoping it goes well. I need to stop clinging to this notion that I've had lately that Tiffany and I are going to end up together. This idea that she's going to fall in love with me, leave her husband, and move to London is ridiculous. So I want tonight to go well because I can't keep living in this Groundhog Day where I wake up, go to work, and pine after her.

I get off at Tottenham Court Road station and walk up the steps. I scan the area looking for a woman who seems as if she's waiting for someone. There are a couple of tourists arguing over the directions the GPS on their phone is taking them. I spot a woman standing outside a restaurant looking around. She's tall, slim, got brown hair and wearing a black skirt, a white T-shirt, and a black leather jacket, topped off with a pair of thick Doc Martens. She pulls it off really well; it's more stylish than it is steampunk. As I get closer, I see her face. She's very pretty, in a casual way, not in a plastered-makeup way.

"Hi, are you Margaret's daughter?" I ask, realizing Mum never gave me her name.

"Yes, I'm Rain," she replies.

"Nice to meet you," I say, holding my hand out for her to shake it.

"Shall we go inside?" she asks.

I nod, before following a woman who is named after a weather forecast that nobody likes, for a blind date that up to 2 hours ago, I didn't know I was having.

A waiter shows us to our table. I instinctively go to pull the chair out for her.

"No!" she almost yells at me. "There'll be none of that thank you. It's 2024."

Like I wasn't aware of the year.

"Sorry," I say, taken aback.

"And there'll be no ordering wine for the table either. I can choose my own drink."

What a fantastic start, I think to myself.

I order a beer, she orders an elderflower cocktail, and the waiter goes away to fetch the drinks.

I look around the restaurant. It's very small, very quiet, and the walls are littered with colourful drawings. It looks like a children's nursery.

"I'm sorry about before," she says, softening.

"I don't believe in all that alpha male bullshit. I wouldn't have gotten to where I am in my field if I'd bought into a male-dominated world, where the man chases after the woman and she swoons like some damsel in distress."

I'm not sure what she does for a living, but after that speech, I'm guessing the army.

"What do you do for a living?" I ask, desperately trying to divert her away from her rant.

"I'm a marine biologist, and despite reports that it is a male-dominated field, 60% of marine biologists are female, so like I said, I don't buy into that bullshit. I work primarily studying eels, and here's an interesting fact for you," she says.

I can't wait for this, I think to myself, because so far nothing she has said has held any interest.

"Moray eels are not aggressive when they open and close their mouths; they are actually just breathing," she says, excitedly.

I do my best to feign excitement. I look like someone who's received a Christmas present they've already received three of.

"I also do some volunteer work," she continues. "Do you do any volunteer work?"

"I wouldn't do volunteer work if you paid me," I reply.

"But you wouldn't get paid, it's volunteer work," she says, completely missing the joke.

The waiter comes back with our drinks and asks us if we are ready to order. It's then that I realize I haven't even looked at the menu.

"What steaks do you do?" I ask him.

"We don't do steak, I'm afraid. This is a vegan restaurant," he answers.

Of course, it is, I think to myself.

I look at the menu.

"Okay, I will have a vegan cheese and tomato pizza," I say, playing it safe.

"And for the lady," the waiter says, and I think he's about to get an earful, but she ignores it.

"I will have the grilled asparagus and courgettes please," she replies.

The waiter disappears into the back. She talks about eels for another 20 minutes before asking me what I do for a living.

I tell her the basics, because I'm not really allowed to discuss the new project, and by the looks of her face, she's not that interested anyway. There's a bit of silence, so we both take a sip of our drinks.

"Who did you vote for in the last local election?" she asks after a few minutes.

"I don't vote."

"What do you mean you don't vote?" she asks, astounded.

"I mean I don't go down to some Methodist church and tick a box," I reply sarcastically.

"What do you do then?"

"I stay at home," I laugh.

Her face is thunder. Great, now I've really wound her up.

"Don't you care about the state of the country?" she snaps.

"Of course I do, but it doesn't seem to matter who's running it, they are pretty much all the same."

"So if you're not interested in politics, what are you interested in?"

"I mainly just listen to music or read," I reply.

"So, can I ask you a question? And I don't mean to be rude."

Which up to this point, she's been nothing but rude, so it wouldn't exactly change anything. I think to myself as she carries on.

"Do you think you read and listen to music to escape the harsh realities of what's going on in the world?"

"Well yeah, doesn't everybody?" I reply.

"I mean, everybody reads or watches TV or listens to music. But they're also clued up with what's going on and get involved to try and make a difference," she counters.

"First of all, not everybody gets involved and tries to make a difference. (I use air quotes for the word difference) I t's a personal preference. At least my way sounds fun; yours just sounds depressing."

The waiter comes out with the food, and his timing is so perfect I could kiss him. He puts the pizza down, and I take a bite out of a slice. You know when you buy a pizza from a supermarket, and it comes on that piece of cardboard the same size as the pizza? Well this vegan pizza tastes like the chef accidentally cooked the cardboard bit. It's blander than a doctor's waiting room. I've decided that after I've finished eating, I'm going to call it a night. But rain beats me to it. I haven't even finished chewing my last slice when she tells me she's got an early start and she better go. It's music to my ears, and I ask the waiter for the bill.

"Who wants the bill?" he asks when he comes back to the table. Rain points at me.

"So let me get this straight," I say, laughing, at the farce that is the whole evening.

"You wouldn't let me get your chair for you, or order wine for the table. You gave me a speech about it being 2024, and that you don't believe a man should chase a woman, and yet the bill comes and you want me to pay? Surely you can't be serious."

It's not that I begrudge paying, but it's the principle of the matter. She looks at me sheepishly.

"You invited me out, it's only right that you should pay," she says. "But I didn't invite you out, I didn't even know anything about it until 5 o'clock tonight. You know what, it's fine." I say, desperate for this date to be over.

I pay the bill and get out of my chair. I can feel her following behind me as I walk to the exit and out onto the pavement.

"Bye, Rob," she says, walking away before I can say anything.

I start making my way back to the tube station, and just when I think I've had enough of rain, it pisses it down.

9. Cloud Chasing

Saturday 6th July 2024

After last night's fiasco and the inedible pizza, I'm having a bacon butty and listening to BBC 6. I'm anticipating a call from Mum at some point to ask me how it went, and I really don't know what to tell her.
 One thing I do know though, is that I'm not yet ready to date. It wasn't just because the date was horrendous, but it's only been 4 months and it just seems too early. The phone rings, and I'm expecting it to be Mum, but it's Paul.
 "Hi mate, what are you up to today?" he asks.
 "Not a lot really. I was going to nip to the bookshop to see if they've got anything new and maybe pick up some stuff on the way home to make a spaghetti Bolognese," I reply.
 "Rock and roll Saturday then," he laughs.
 "I was thinking, I've got a spare ticket to Wimbledon if you fancy it. Andy has bailed on me," he adds.
 "Wimbledon really!" I say, struggling to hide the excitement in my voice. "I'd love to go."
 "Are you a fan then?"
 "Are you kidding me? I'm a massive fan," I beam.
 This is the first thing I've done since Michelle left that I know she would be jealous of.
 We used to watch Wimbledon every year at her mum and dad's, and they would do a proper Wimbledon party with Pimms, scones with clotted cream and jam, and strawberries and cream.
 "Where are the seats?" I ask, even though I'm not bothered where they are.
 "Centre."
 "Centre! That's amazing, what time?"
 "3 o'clock, but meet me before and we will go for a pint," he says.
 "Ok see you then," I say excitedly.

I can't believe I'm going to watch Wimbledon. On centre court as well.
I have to ring Dad.
He picks up after three rings.
"Dad, guess where I'm going today?"
"I don't know, Rob. Where are you going today?"
"Is that our Rob!" Mum shouts from the kitchen.
"Of course it is!" he shouts back. "We don't know any other Robs."
"Ask him how his date went," comes Mum's voice again.
"No, Mary, I won't!" he yells back. "You'll have to find out on Tuesday when you see Margaret."
"Sorry son, where are you going?"
"Wimbledon Centre Court. You might even see me on TV."
"You jammy git!" he replies.
"Well, enjoy yourself son, and take plenty of photos," he adds before we end the call.
I look at the weather and it's going to be scorching, so I stick on a pair of Chino shorts and a polo shirt.
I'm meeting Paul at Earls Court, but we've got to get from Earls Court to Wimbledon, which takes around 30 minutes. So that's 50 minutes in total from King's Cross. I leave at 12.00 pm to be safe. On the walk to the tube station, I'm listening to "Porcelain" by Moby. It's a downtempo chill-out piano track, and when that's all you can hear, and the weather is beaming, it's so serene. I meet Paul, and I follow him to the platform that will take us to Wimbledon. We both manage to get a seat but the tube is packed, so we are quite a bit away from each other. I go back to listening to music. In the half an hour it takes to get to the station closest to Wimbledon, I listen to songs from:

- Foo Fighters

- Laura Marling

- The Strokes

- The Chemical Brothers

- Joy Division

- Chicane

- My Chemical Romance

- The Streets

The best thing about music is that it's subjective. You can take the most popular bands in the world and you'll still find thousands of people who don't like them. Those thousands of people aren't wrong, or right for that matter. It's all about taste. And I genuinely believe that every genre of music has the ability to be good, as long as it's done properly. Music is also one of the most powerful things we have in the world. You can take every single moment of your life and soundtrack it. It's no wonder we meticulously choose what song we are going to dance to at our weddings and what songs we want to be buried to at our funerals. It tells a story of the type of people we are and the lives we've lived.

Paul comes walking over and tells me the next stop is our stop, and before I know it the tube is slowing down. We make our way out of the station.

"We haven't got time for a pint," he says, disappointed.

"But I do need to nip into the vape shop; I'm running out of juice." I follow him to a place called Leon's vape shop, and it couldn't be clearer. It's a vape shop owned by a bloke called Leon, and by the looks of it, it's only big enough for just Leon himself to work there.

Seriously, the max capacity is five at a push.

"Hi, can I help you?" he asks as we enter.

"Yeah, have you got anything fruity?" Paul replies.

"Yeah, we've actually got three new fruit flavours. We've got Dragon's Punch, which is grape. The Magician's Nephew, which is watermelon, and the Flamethrower's Compass, which is blueberry," he says.

Why he couldn't have just said we've got grape, watermelon, and blueberry, I'll never know.

"I'll take two bottles of the magician's nephew," Paul says, completely unfazed by the ridiculousness of the conversation.

"And what about you?" Leon says, turning to me. "See anything you like?"

I decide to play along.

"Well, I've never vaped before, so what would you recommend?" I ask.

"Well, it all depends. Do you want to be a cloud chaser?" he replies.

"I can honestly say no one has ever asked me that. What is it?" I reply, even more confused than when I walked in.

"Cloud chasing is where you blow large, long clouds from your vape, and if you want to do that, you will need the Geekvape T200 Kit, which will set you back around £75. Now, I haven't actually got one in stock, but I can put you in touch with my mate Alan who owns a vape shop in Soho?"

"No, it's okay. I live near Soho. I'll nip in and have a chat with him," I say, having no intention of going anywhere near the shop.

After the vape shop, we walk for about 20 minutes, and that's when I see the sign. *Welcome to Plough Lane, Home of AFC Wimbledon Football Club.*

"When you said Wimbledon, I thought you meant tennis," I say, disappointed.

"You've got to be kidding haven't you? Do you know how hard it is to get tickets for that? You've got to be either filthy rich or a royal. Do you not like football?" he asks.

"Yeah I do," I reply.

It's not a total lie. I know all the rules, but I don't watch club football. I only watch England when it's the World Cup.

We show our tickets and walk through the turnstile. We walk up the concrete steps that never seem to end and out into the stands. We settle into our seats. The sun is beaming onto the pitch and everyone's anticipating kick-off. The teams come out, and it's AFC Wimbledon vs Blackburn. Both teams take their positions, and the referee blows the whistle to start the game. 5 minutes in and the Wimbledon fans are in full voice. Singing about how they are the greatest team the world has ever seen. 5 minutes go by and I'm really getting into the game. But it's a strange sensation watching a football match live because you only get to see things once, there are no replays, so if you blink you miss it. There's also no commentator, so you really are on your own. Wimbledon fans are now singing about how much they hate Milton Keynes Dons, which is really strange because I thought they were playing Blackburn.

"Why are they singing about Milton Keynes?" I ask Paul, who's not really spoken since the game Kicked off.

"They are our rivals and we don't like them," he answers.

"Fair enough," I say, but it's pretty pointless as there are no Milton Keynes supporters here to hear it.

"Is this an important game?" I ask.

"No, it's only a friendly," he replies, chewing his nails.

The first half flies by. It's 0-0, but it's a good game so far. There are plenty of oohs and aahs from the crowd, and you can't help but get sucked into it all.

At halftime, Paul goes off to get us both a beer. I stay seated and watch the club mascot parade around the pitch. Paul returns with two cold pints in plastic glasses, and we talk about the first half.

When the game kicks off again, one of the Blackburn players goes flying into one of the Wimbledon players, studs first, and both sets of fans react. There's a bit of commotion right near us. Three men in bright-coloured tracksuits are cursing the Wimbledon fans. They look like JD Sports mannequins. You know the type of blokes I'm talking about. The type of blokes where the only record they own is a criminal one. Worst of all, they are all over 40. It really is embarrassing. How do they wake up on a Saturday, put on a full tracksuit, look in the mirror, and think, "I can't wait to get tanked up and really give it to a group of people who have worked all week and paid good money to come and watch their local team." Instantly I now want Wimbledon to win more than ever.

It's amazing how a few fans can make you hate an entire team and fan base. The game is coming to an end and the score is 0-0 with about 3 minutes left. The referee gives Wimbledon a penalty and everyone around me cheers like it's already in.

It's a pre season friendly, it means nothing in terms of points, but I've never wanted someone to score as much as I do now. The Wimbledon player steps up and hammers the ball so hard he nearly breaks the goal.

Chaos erupts around me. Paul is grabbing me and I can't help but celebrate with him. The referee blows the whistle. The celebrations continue outside the ground. We go to the pub for a few drinks afterwards.

"You enjoyed yourself today didn't you?" Paul asks me, smiling.

"I did, but I've got one question to ask you: what's it like when the game actually means something?"

"You have no idea," he replies.

10. Soulmates

Monday 5th August 2024

After a month of late nights, split opinions, a few heated debates (mainly between Paul and Andy), and the writing and almost rewriting of everything we'd done since the start, we are nearly finished. Last Friday we went through the checklist.

Objective

Format

Message

Timing

Target audience

Bottle shape

Advertisement

Music for the advertisement

Actors/actresses

In regards to the advert, we decided to go with Tiffany's idea of staying away from the celebrated, fashionable notion that sex sells. Instead of going with the traditional advert of a male actor lying on a bed with his shirt off, or the said male actor walking out of the sea wearing nothing but a pair of budgie smugglers, with abs you could iron your clothes on. our actor Dominic Moon, (whom I can't believe we've managed to book, considering only last week he was tipped to be the next James Bond,) has got a big job interview. He puts on the aftershave before putting on his suit, and what follows is a slow-motion shot of him walking confidently through a crowded street on his way to the interview. Soft, chilled-out music plays as he walks into the office. He emerges sometime later, smiling and shaking the interviewer's hand before walking out.

The message that we want to convey is that putting on our product gives you the confidence to go after the things you want.

Steve has told us that he's taking care of the venue location and will let us know when it's confirmed. It's Monday morning, and I arrive at the office before the rest of the team. I flick the kettle on, put a tea bag and one sugar in a cup. It used to be two, but I'm trying to cut it down. Paul arrives 5 minutes later with a takeaway coffee. We chat about the weekend. I haven't done anything with him on a weekend since the match.

We've both been busy. He's been going to the gym with Andy. They invited me, but I refuse to pay £50 a month to run when I can run in the streets for free. On the subject of running, I need to start going again. All this beer is giving me an even bigger beer belly.

Two weeks ago, I took Mum out for her 65th birthday, and for the last few Sundays, I've been playing golf with Dad. I told him about the Wimbledon mix-up, and I think he was more disappointed than I was.

Andy arrives, makes himself a coffee, and joins the two of us.

We chat for only a minute or so before Steve walks through the door, takes his seat, and asks us to do the same.

"Right, we are all here," he says adjusting his tie.

"What about Tiffany?" Andy asks, as confused as I am.

"She's gone back to Rome," he replies, like it was obvious.

"What!" I say, shell-shocked.

I'm about to protest further but stop myself. I don't want them to know how much I like her and that I'm not just asking from a colleague's point of view.

"I'll explain if you let me," he says, annoyed at the interruption. "Now, as you know, we are so close to being completely finished. The only things left to do are choose a venue and shoot the advert. I've spoken to Luca Amato, and he wants to shoot the advert in Rome. As you also know, Tiffany works and lives in Rome, so because there's nothing left to do here, she's gone home to resume the duties she had before this project started, which is also what I would like you three to do here. Luca has chosen April/May to shoot the advert. So, if you haven't got an in-date passport, you've got until April to get one."

He sees the look on our faces before carrying on. "We need you three and Tiffany on set. Writing a manuscript for an advertisement is one thing, but it needs to be filmed just as we've all imagined. We still need you to find a location in Rome for the shoot. I will be in touch with dates, flights, and your accommodation. I can't go because I've got to be here. Which I'm devastated about, but it can't be helped. I would like to say thank you for all your hard work. And when it's all over, I will be taking you all out to celebrate."

He finishes and leaves the conference room.

"Fucking hell. We are going to Rome. How cool is that?" Andy squeals excitedly.

I'm trying so hard not to look so disappointed with the fact that I'm not going to see Tiffany until at least April.

"The Colosseum, The Trevi Fountain, the Vatican, pizza, pasta, lasagne, ice cream. I can't wait," Paul adds.

I go back to my office for the first time in ages, and I sit in my chair. I can't shake this feeling I've got. It's like somebody has ripped apart of me away. Which is stupid because the feelings I've got for her aren't reciprocated. She's only ever going to see me as this bloke who she worked on a project with. It's probably a good thing she's gone back. I might finally stop this ridiculous fantasy.

By Friday I've settled back into the work routine I had before starting the project. The only difference is I've started having my dinner with Paul and Andy, which is great because I need the company. I'm so bored working in my office on my own. "Fancy coming out for a meal tonight with me and Paul?" Andy asks, as he bites into a cheese and onion roll.
"Yeah, can do," I say, between chews of my own sandwich.
"Dress smart, though, it's a posh place," he adds.
"How smart?"
"Well, not suit smart, but a shirt instead of a t-shirt, and shoes instead of trainers," he replies.
"Where is it and what time?"
"Brixton, be there for 6;30," he replies.

When I get out of Brixton station, I spot Paul and Andy waiting for me. They are both dressed the smartest I've ever seen them. They've both got shirts on, and Andy has even done his hair, we head towards the restaurant.
From the outside, it doesn't look posh; it doesn't even look like a restaurant, It looks more like a pub.
We go inside and it is a pub, and 2 yards from the entrance, there's a woman sitting at a table. She sees us walk in. 'Welcome to the Green Dragon, singles' night, speed dating,' she says excitedly.
Most people have a bucket list: things like bungee jumping, climbing Mount Everest, swimming with dolphins, and going on a cruise.
But is there a bucket list for the things you've been tricked into doing? Because my life is slowly becoming a slapstick comedy. I stand there in the pub and replay the events of the last 6 months. I've participated in a hot dog eating competition, gone on a blind date with a politically obsessed vegan, been to a football match

when I thought I was going to the tennis, and now I'm speed dating.

Yet none of this would have happened if Michelle hadn't left me. I have to admit, though. Apart from the blind date, I have enjoyed myself.

All the things I've done with Andy and Paul have been hilarious experiences. over the last couple of months, I've been telling myself that I'm not ready to date. But being with someone, has got to be better than being alone.

Some people say a single life is great. You can go wherever you want and do whatever you want, and the only person you have to consider is yourself. And I'm happy for them.

But the more nights I come home to an empty house, the more those deep-seated feelings of loneliness consume me. It's amazing how adding just one other person to an empty room can make it feel massive.

But above all, it's the little things I miss. Like watching a film and discussing it in detail with someone once it's finished, or coming home and someone just asking you if you've had a nice day?

So I decide to go ahead and participate. I mean, what's the worst that can happen?

"Name, age, and occupation," the woman behind the table says to me like I'm checking in at the doctors.

"Rob Swan, 28, marketing." She jots it down and turns to Paul.

"Paul Fields, 33, marketing." Finally, she turns to Andy.

"Lance Green, 26, lifeguard," he says.

Paul and I share the same look of confusion but say nothing.

She gives us our name tags and tells us the room we are going to be in is to the left. We go through to the bar and order a pint before taking a seat at a table in the corner.

"Lance Green," I say, laughing.

"I didn't want to give my real name," he says.

"Why not?" I ask, thinking maybe I shouldn't have given mine.

"Because at these things, you can be anyone you want, and I didn't want to be Andy Parks, 34, in marketing. I wanted to be Lance Green, 26, a lifeguard who is also brilliant at DIY and can cook."

The room starts to fill up with fellow singletons. We get a look at the females we are going to be chatting with.

"By the way, we are going to see a David Bowie tribute band tomorrow night, in Soho. If you want to come?" Paul asks, sipping his drink.

"Is it actually a gig though?" I ask wearily. "Or is it another one of those things, where it ends up being something else like tonight?"

They both smile.

"No, we promise it's a gig. They are called Simply Bowie, they are really good."

"Then yeah, that would be amazing," I say excitedly.

We manage to have two more drinks each and order a fourth before the woman comes through with a clipboard.

"Right, everybody," she yells around the room. "This is how it's going to work. You will get 3 minutes to chat with each participant. There are two rows of eight chairs – fellas on the left, ladies on the right. When your 3 minutes are up, the fellas move down the row while the ladies stay seated. If you're at the bottom of the row, you move to the seat at the top. If by the end someone sparks your interest, you write your name down and the other person's name down, and hand it in. If two people write each other's names down, you will be matched. Any questions?"

Nobody says anything, so she takes that as a no, and one by one we make our way to a seat. I'm seated in the 3rd chair from the top. Andy (Lance) is to my left, and Paul is to the right, but further down. I'm sitting opposite a small woman with a brown bob haircut and glasses. She looks a bit like Thelma from Scooby-Doo. Her name tag says Shelly. She smiles at me, and I smile back.

"Your first 3 minutes start now!" she yells.

"Hi, I'm Rob," I say, which is a ridiculous thing to say because it clearly says it on my name tag. "What do you do for a living Shelly?" I ask.

For the next 2 minutes and 40 seconds, she tells me that she's an accountant and how stressful it can be. She finally asks me what I do, and 20 seconds later the woman shouts "Time's up, move to your next singleton."

I shuffle down and can't get over how ridiculous this is. 3 minutes is nowhere near enough time to have a conversation with someone.

My next date is Rachel, who has black hair, brown eyes, a crooked nose, and a tattoo of a magpie on her wrist. The time starts and she speaks very softly, so softly in fact that I can't really hear what she's saying. All I can hear is the conversation between Andy (Lance) and Shelly, whom I've just had a date with.

"You don't look like a lifeguard," she says.

"That's because Baywatch has ruined people's perception of lifeguards. We don't all look like David Hasselhoff," he replies.

"How many people have you saved?"

"Too many to count."

"What does that feel like?"

"You don't have time to feel. When someone's in danger the adrenaline just takes over," he replies.

Before I know it my time with Rachel is over and I don't really know what's been said.

Next up is date number 3: Gabrielle.

"Cats or dogs?" she asks.

"Erm, cats," I reply.

"Me too," she smiles.

"TV shows or films?"

"TV shows."

"Me too."

"Chinese food or Indian food?"

"Indian food."

"Oh my god, me too! We have so much in common. You're like my soul mate," she squeals.

I want to say, *Not really. You've asked me three 50-50 questions, and they just so happen to be the same answers you would have given. That doesn't make us soul mates.* But I don't.

"I know this is going to sound forward, but my sister is getting married next month, would you like to be my date?"

Now it makes sense. No matter what answers I'd given, they would have been the same as hers, because she was just looking for someone to go to her sister's wedding with. I ask her when it is to be polite and tell her I can't make it I'm busy that day. She gives me a look of disbelief because it's probably the same answer she's just had from the last date. When it's time to move seats, I sit opposite Rebecca. She has Long brown hair, olive skin, tiny fragments of a dimple beside each cheek. I go to speak but she quickly holds her hand up to stop me. Looks like this one is over before it's started. "We've only got 3 minutes. Don't talk, just listen. My name isn't Rebecca. You won't find out my real name," she says, like she works for MI5 and my life is in danger.

"I've looked around this room and out of all the 8 men, you are the most attractive. My job is exhausting and I love it, but it gives me no time to date people. But like everyone else, I have needs. I'm in London for one more night. I'm staying at the Hilton Hotel down the street, room 302. If you are interested in a night of fun, no talking, no getting to know each other, no exchanging details, or looking each other up on social media, come to my room. Have a think about it." She finishes talking, and I don't say a word. I'm bewildered.

The next 4 dates follow a similar pattern as the first three because like I said, three minutes just isn't long enough to get to know a person. When it's all over I don't write anybody's name down. Paul writes one down and Andy writes two. Andy doesn't get a match. It seems the lifeguard act didn't work. But Paul gets matched and it's nice to see how excited he is. Turns out it was Shelly that he gets matched with, and he goes off with her, which I'm guessing to a proper date. I sit at the bar with Andy and we swap stories of our dates. I don't tell him about the proposition I got. After a few more drinks, I'm at the stage that really defines your level of drunkenness. Leave it as it is and I'll be fine, but one more could be consequential. Andy seems to have the same realization. "I'm going to call it a night," he says, getting up off his stool. I look at my pint and it's three-quarters full.

"I'm going to stay and finish this," I say.

Andy leaves, and I'm on my own. I drink the rest of the pint, head out the door, and make my way to the Hilton hotel.

11. Snakebite.

"So, what happened next?" Paul asks me over the phone, hanging onto my every word as if I'm describing an episode of a Netflix drama.
"I got to the hotel room and was about to knock, but I couldn't go through with it, as tempting as it was," I reply, regretfully.
"What made you change your mind?"
"Well, as I was walking down the hallway, reading the room numbers trying to find 302, it occurred to me. What if I perform terribly? My whole life I've only been with one woman, Michelle, and when you're in a relationship for that long you know each other's likes and dislikes. It's comfortable and easy. But this woman was brash and honest, she knew exactly what she wanted. What if I couldn't give her what she wanted?"
"But you never would have seen her again," he says when I've finished."
I know, but it still would have been emasculating," I say. "Anyway, how was your date?" I ask, which was the reason he was calling me in the first place, to tell me about it.
"Yeah, it went well. So well in fact, that I'm seeing her next weekend," he replies.

****

I arrive at Mum and Dad's around midday. As I walk into the house, I hear Mum's raised voice and I guess she's telling Dad off for something. Then I start to make out what's being said and realize she's not talking to Dad at all. "What's the point in you coming to book club Margaret if you're three chapters behind?" she yells from the kitchen.
"I've been going to bingo. I haven't had time to read it. I won £100 the other day," Margaret proudly answers.
"I don't care if you won £100,000. You took an oath," my mum shouts, getting louder.

"An oath? It's a book club Mary, I'm not giving evidence in court. Besides, I didn't see you complaining when you were tucking into those £4 Marks and Spencer's sausage rolls I brought around."

I walk through the living room and into the kitchen; it smells like someone's spilled red wine on an Avon catalogue. The five women turn to face me.

"Hiya, Rob darling," my mum says, turning from Hyde back to Jekyll.

"So this is the Rob that yelled at my daughter because she wanted the man to pay, which surely is customary and traditional," Margaret says snidely.

I laugh to myself but don't respond. I've always been one of those people who doesn't care what others think as long as I know the truth. Margaret can go on thinking what she wants. I won't lose any sleep over it.

"Dad outside?" I ask Mum directly, which I know will anger Margaret more.

"Yes, darling. You go through and see him and I'll talk to you soon." I hear her telling Margaret she can come back if she gets up to date with the book, and I leave them to it. I go outside and see that the side door to the garage is open, so I go inside. My dad is sitting in the corner in his chair, with his eyes closed and his headphones on. At first I think he's asleep, but then his face changes to a look of pure joy. It's the look he gets when a song comes on that he loves, and he loses himself in it. I stand there for a minute and really look at him. At 67 years old, he's starting to look his age. He has this weather-beaten face that a lot of builders get from working long hours in the cold. But I also see a man who knows exactly what he wants, and those things are not the world; they are the simple pleasures like a good book or a new record. Let him have that, and he's happy. He opens his eyes, sees me, and smiles before taking off his headphones. "Hello son, how are you?" he asks.

"I'm fine, thanks dad. How are you?"

"I'm alright now that I'm away from the madhouse," he says, laughing. "So what's new?" he adds.

"I'm going to see a David Bowie tribute act in Soho tonight. I can't wait. I've never been to a gig before."

"Take me with you," he replies, only half-joking. I tell him about the speed dating and leave out the bit about the mysterious woman and the hotel. There are just some things you shouldn't tell your parents. When I finish, he looks at me and says, "Dating in this day and age sounds like a minefield. I don't envy you one bit, son." He makes me a cup of tea and we sit and chat about music and books. We don't even scratch the surface. I could sit there all day and talk to him about it. When the book club has finished and everyone has gone home, we go back into the house. Mum is in the kitchen tidying up. She asks me if I'm hungry. I say that I am, so she microwaves me some leftover Shepherd's pie.

"I need to tell you both something," I say between mouthfuls. "I'm going to Rome for a few weeks to find a venue and shoot the advert for the new aftershave."

"Very nice," Dad says.

"Can you bring us back a fridge magnet?" Mum adds. And that's it, that's all they say. Around 4 o'clock, I leave to go home and get ready.

****

I've showered and I'm contemplating what to wear. Dad told me earlier that it's an unwritten rule that you don't wear a t-shirt of the band/artist you are going to see, so I throw on a Nirvana t-shirt, a pair of black skinny jeans, and some Vans before getting the tube to Soho to meet Andy and Paul. I can feel the excitement building as we make our way to the venue. When we get there, I notice two queues. One is for tickets already bought, and the other is for people who are paying at the door. We join the latter queue and slowly make our way inside. Andy buys three tickets. I ask him how much I owe him, and he tells me it was only a tenner and to just buy him a drink inside.

We go inside, and the place is like a dimly lit basement full of strobe lighting. There's a small stall of the band's merchandise on one side and a bar on the other. At the top, all around the sides, is the balcony area. The level we are on is one big open floor with a stage at the back, separated by a metal barrier. I queue up to get the three of us a beer. The place is heaving and there's a vibrant buzz around. I get three pints of beer in plastic cups and carry them over to Andy and Paul. Andy tells me we've missed the support band, and I can't help feeling a little bit gutted. I wanted to experience all of it. "Come on, I want to get to the front," Paul says to both of us, leading the way forward and squeezing his way through a crowd of people. Andy follows behind him.

I hear a few people tut and moan, so I decide to stay here close to the bar, out of the way of everyone. I don't need to be at the front; it's fine. Music plays over the speakers while the stage crew sets up equipment and test microphones. I look to my left and realize I'm quite close to the ladies' toilets. I've never seen so many women in jeans and Converse. I need to avert my gaze somewhere else; otherwise, they will think I'm some sort of pervert who hangs around the ladies' toilets.

Hang on a minute, I think to myself, *is that Tiffany? It does look like her*—she's wearing a New York Dolls t-shirt, blue jeans, and some low Converse trainers. It is her, I'm sure of it. She looks to her right and spots me, and I think for a minute that her face lights up. It's probably from the shock of seeing me, but she definitely doesn't look unhappy. "ROB," she shouts, throwing her arms around me before kissing me on the cheek. It's the first bit of female interaction I've had in months, even if it is just a friendly greeting.

"What are you doing here? I thought you'd gone back to Italy," I ask, stunned.

"My flight's not till Monday, so I thought I'd have a night out instead of sitting in that hotel room for another night."

"Who are you with?" she asks. I can see she's had a few drinks.
"Paul and Andy, but they are down the front somewhere," I reply.
"So, have you seen these before then?" she asks.
"I've never been to a gig before," I say regretfully.
"WHAT? NEVER?"
I shake my head.
"Oh, Rob. That's really upset me, that has," like I'd just told her I had months to live. "Right. Well, if this is your first gig, we are doing it properly." She takes my hand, leads me to the bar, and tells me to wait for her to come back. She fights her way to the front. I see her hold up 2 fingers to the bartender. He makes 2 drinks, she gives him the money, and she comes back over with 2 massive plastic cups of purple liquid.
"What is it? And why is it so big?" I ask, a little bit scared of what's in it. "It's a snakebite and black. Half beer, half cider, and blackcurrant, and it's a 2-pinter. You can't start a gig without one; it's an unwritten rule." There seem to be a lot of unwritten rules to these things. I take a sip of the snakebite, and it weirdly tastes quite nice. My reaction seems to please Tiffany.
"Right then, let's get to the front," she demands. She takes my hand again, and we are off through the gauntlet of people, within 5 yards of the metal barrier. She checks her phone. "It's 8:30. According to the poster I saw on the way in, we've got half an hour till the band comes on," she claims. "So we are going to play a drinking game," she adds.
"Okay," I say eagerly.
At this point, she could tell me to jump on stage and do an acoustic set, and I would.
"Right, the music playing for the next half an hour will be songs by bands and artists similar to David Bowie, we will both try to guess who the next artist is. If one of us gueses the correct artist the other person has to drink" we play the game for the next 25 minutes and we both manage to get one right each. As the last song starts to

fade, the room plunges into darkness except for one purple neon light that consumes the stage. A man dressed as Ziggy Stardust saunters on after them and takes his place behind the microphone. The place is silent. He's got the whole crowd in his hands, waiting for him. He readies himself. "I'M AN ALLIGATOR!" he yells into the mic, and as he does, a guitar pierces through every speaker and reverberates around the whole room. It doesn't sound tinny or distorted; it sounds perfect. "I'M A MAMA-PAPA COMING FOR YOU," he continues. The place erupts. Plastic cups, half full, fly everywhere. One of them misses me by inches. I look at Tiffany, and she looks like she's been possessed, her arms flaying everywhere. She looks back at me and gives me this look as if to say, "Rob, you are in a safe space here. If you want to sing your heart out, do it. If you want to dance until your legs give way, it's fine. Don't worry about how you might look; no one is paying attention to you." So I do. I mimic the people around me, and before I know it, I'm fully immersed. The song ends, and the next one begins immediately, and it's "Rebel Rebel." And it's rinse and repeat, but this time Tiffany turns to me, and our faces are about 5 inches apart. I think about what it would be like to kiss her. We are yelling the words at each other while moving our hips at the same time. It's the most exhilarating thing I've ever experienced, and this is only a cover band. I can only imagine what it would be like to go see a genuine one. When a slow song comes on, Tiffany tells me she's nipping to the loo and that she will be back. All I can do is hope she does. Now that I've stopped dancing, I realize I'm sweating buckets. But I look around and see that everyone else is too. I check my phone and see I have two missed calls and a message from Andy, which simply reads, "Where are you?" I ignore them. I know it sounds pathetic, but I want Tiffany all to myself. I know nothing is going to happen, but I'm just enjoying the moment. Tiffany comes back carrying two pints of beer and hands me one. For the next few songs, we stand sipping our drinks and just appreciate the musicians on stage. I look over at her. She has this permanent smile plastered across her face. And all I can think of is how amazing she is. The next song is "Gene Genie." Tiffany looks at me and quickly finishes the rest of her drink, so she can dance. I'm so determined to do the same that I don't notice a scuffle between two men behind me until I'm on the floor, and the heavier one has landed on my shoulder. Tiffany looks for me and sees me on the floor. A look of anguish crosses my face. Even with a few pints in me, I'm in a lot of pain.

"Are you okay?" Tiffany asks as I get up.

"I'm fine," I reply, but my face and tone say otherwise. I try to lift my arm up, and the pain sears through my shoulder, causing me to let out a groan loud enough for her to hear me. "Come on," she says, "let's get you outside."

12. Scotch Egg?

Sunday, 11th August, 2024.

We go outside, and Tiffany tells me to sit on the wall. I do as I'm told. Despite the fact that it's a mild night, I can feel the coldness of the concrete through my jeans. Tiffany is by the curb attempting to flag down a taxi. When one arrives, I amble over to her. She opens the door for me and guides me in before getting in herself.
"Where to?" the driver asks, yawning.
"The hospital," Tiffany replies, which is a shock to me because I thought she was sending me home.
"And where are you going?" I ask her.
"I'm coming with you," she replies, like it was obvious.
"But what about the gig?" I ask, hoping she doesn't change her mind.
"It's only a tribute band, Rob. I mean, if it was the Thin White Duke himself, I'd have to reconsider, but I can't let you go on your own."
I smile to myself as I sit back, and for the briefest moment, I forget all about the pain.

We arrive at the hospital, and I pay the driver. Tiffany gets the door for me. We walk through the automatic doors. If it's possible, the waiting room is busier than the gig we've just been to. We go to the receptionist who's sitting behind a thin layer of glass.
"How can I help?" she asks, probably for the hundredth time tonight.
"It's my friend," Tiffany replies. "We were at a gig and someone landed on his shoulder." Upon hearing the word 'friend,' I don't know how I feel. A part of me is gutted that I'm only her friend, but the other part of me is glad she didn't say work colleague. The receptionist tells us to take a seat, and we manage to find two in the corner next to a woman who must be in her 70s. Tiffany can

sense I'm in pain, so she talks to me to take my mind off my shoulder.

"Did you enjoy the gig then?" she asks.

"I loved it, apart from ending up here. It was amazing. I can't wait to do it again," I reply. Nurses come out and call names, and I listen carefully for mine. There's a man in a gown pacing up and down, unable to sit, a kid in a wheelchair with his foot elevated, wearing only one sock, and a woman with a disposable sick bowl, among other patients. The automatic doors open, and a policeman escorts a lad no older than 20 in; he's struggling to stand up. He's had that much to drink. It makes me think of what Mum and Dad went through the night they got the phone call, that Jason had overdosed. We talked some more about the gig and what to expect when I come over to Rome in April. An hour passes, and I still haven't even had my name called. Tiffany yawns and I really don't want her to go. A nurse comes out of one of the double doors with a clipboard.

"Can I have everybody's attention?" she yells. Everybody stops what they are doing and listens. "I'm going to do a quick roll call. If you hear your name, put your hand up or say 'here' like it's a school assembly." She rattles off the names and patients respond. I don't hear mine. She goes to walk away, but I manage to catch her before she goes.

"Excuse me, I didn't hear my name," I say, starting to get restless.

"Do you have a red wristband?" she asks. A red wristband? What is this, swimming? or is a red wristband VIP?

"No, I don't. What does a red wristband do?" I ask, completely confused about what's going on.

"A red wristband is for A+E patients," she explains.

"I am an A+E patient," I say, snapping a little bit.

"Not if you don't have a wristband, you're not. You are UTC," she says condescendingly, as if I should know all this.

"Which is what?" I reply, trying so hard not to lose it.

"It stands for Urgent Treatment Centre. We provide medical help when it's not a life-threatening emergency. If you remain seated, we will get you seen to." She turns on her heels and walks away. I sit back down, between Tiffany and the old woman, who turns to me and says, "You've been told your UTC as well, have you?" as if it's some type of disease we both share.

"Yeah," I reply, disappointed.

"I've been up here nearly 2 hours, but luckily I came prepared. Scotch egg?" she says, offering me one from a Tupperware container full of them.

"No, thank you," I say politely, but then I admit to Tiffany that I am hungry. She rifles around her jeans pocket, pulls out a tenner, and tells me she will get us something from the vendor.

"You don't have to do that and you don't have to stay either," I say as she gets out of her chair.

"Don't be silly, I'm partly responsible. This wouldn't have happened if I didn't drag you to the front." I can't remember resisting, I want to say, but don't. She comes back with 2 cups of tea with powdered milk, a packet of cheese and onion crisps, a packet of salt and vinegar crisps, a Mars, and a Snickers, and offers me the choice. I go with salt and vinegar and a Mars because I don't want cheese and onion or peanut breath, and I say thank you.

"What would you say is the easiest job in the world?" she asks as she sits down and opens her packet of crisps. I think for a minute and then say, 'Weatherman.'

"What makes you say that?" she replies, intrigued.

"Think about it, you stand there and tell people what the weather's going to be like. If you happen to get it wrong, no one is going to ring up and complain. They are not going to say, "I'd like to put a complaint in." The weatherman said it wasn't going to rain today. I've put my washing out and it has pissed it down. Are they?"

"Good point," she says, laughing.

"Most boring job then," I say.

Straight away, without any hesitation, she says, "The person who stands at the top of a slide at a water park and tells people when they can go down. Eight hours of just waving people over, that has got to be horrendous."

"Yeah, but think of the tan you'd get," I reply and she laughs again. "How's your shoulder?" she asks and I want to tell her it's fine, but it's still very sore. So I tell her that. "Ok, I've got one for you," she says, getting excited. It's almost as if she's tried to play this game with other people before, but nobody's entertained it. "What's your death row meal? You know, the last meal before you die, and if you say roast dinner, I'm walking out. I don't care how badly your shoulder hurts."

"You don't like roast dinners?" I say, gobsmacked.

"Of course, I do, but come on, no one has veg as their last meal. No one sits there about to die and thinks, "I can't wait to tuck into a nice plate of steamed green broccoli." You get to pick a starter, main, and a pudding," she adds.

"Right, then. For starter, I'm going for tomato soup. For main, I'm going for pie, mash, and gravy, and for pudding, I'm going for a trifle."

"Oh my god, you are so British it hurts," she says after I've finished.

"Ok then, Miss Italia, what are you having?" I say, laughing.

"Starter nachos covered in cheese, salsa, sour cream, and guacamole. Main, a pizza from Rifugio Romano, my favourite restaurant back home, and for pudding, jam roly-poly and custard."

"How good is this pizza?" I ask when she's finished.

"It's the best. I will take you when we are in Rome," she replies.

"It's a date," I say, and I wish I could take the words back as soon as they leave my mouth. "I don't mean it like that," I say backtracking.

"It's fine," she smiles. 'I know what you meant.'

"Mr. Swan," the nurse calls, and I'm finally getting seen. Tiffany stays in the waiting room. I follow the triage nurse to an examination room and get told to take a seat and take off my t-shirt. The nurse presses my shoulder and asks me, 'Does that hurt?' which has got to be the most stupid question I've ever been asked. Of course, it hurts. Why else would I be here? After further examination, she tells me it's dislocated. She tells me to brace myself and pops it back in, and the pain is excruciating for a split second, but that's it. Two and a bit hours later, and I'm apparently fixed, and I can go home. I put my T-shirt back on and go back out into the waiting room. I tell Tiffany, and she's relieved that's all it is. We leave the absolute chaos that is the NHS and head out onto the street.

"Are you going to be alright getting home with your shoulder?" she asks.

"Yeah, I'll be fine," I reply. I don't want this night to end, so I end up blurting out, "Let me buy you breakfast."

"What?" she replies, taken aback.

"Just as a thank you for tonight, there's a cafe around the corner from here that serves breakfast until 2 o'clock in the morning. A nice cup of tea and a bacon butty." I wait in anticipation as she mulls it over.

"Go on then. I am starving," she replies, to my delight. We sit in the cafe for the next hour and drink, eat, and talk. I find out so much more about her. She hates seafood, loves mushrooms. She doesn't eat chicken anymore but sometimes craves a chicken mayo from McDonald's. She hates it when people tap and can't stand seeing men wearing flip-flops. She prefers sweet to savoury, and once she had a dream she was being chased by a Capybara. When she calls it a night, I'm devastated but understand. She gives me a hug and before she goes, she tells me she will see me in April when I come to Rome. I don't want to wish my life away, but it can't come quickly enough.

13. Christmas

4 months later.

Wednesday, the 25th of December.

Time seems to elude me. In the four months since that night at the hospital, it seems that all I've done is eat, drink, work, and sleep. And before I know it, Christmas has crept up on me. I love Christmas. I love everything about it. I love all the songs, except "Band-Aid." That one has always baffled me. There's something about a group of multimillionaires telling working-class people that they don't realize how lucky they are and that they should donate to the less fortunate, that just doesn't seem right. I love the build-up: putting up the Christmas tree, counting down the days on an advent calendar, and watching Christmas films. And the day itself. Michelle waking me up with a cup of tea, wishing each other a merry Christmas, before exchanging gifts. Seeing the look on her face when it's something heartfelt.
  I'm ashamed to say that this year I didn't put a tree up (there didn't seem much point for one person) or get an advent calendar and I've watched the odd Christmas film, but I'm not really getting the Christmas vibes this year. It's partly to do with the fact that Michelle isn't here and Christmas isn't going to be the same on my own and it's also partly down to the fact, that as Christmas day grows closer the crippling fear of seeing my brother for the first time in 10 years gets deeper and deeper. There are so many days I nearly call Mum to tell her I've changed my mind, but end up talking myself out of it.

Christmas day arrives and I'm sitting on the tube on the way to Watford with Mum and Dad's gift. It's a slow cooker which I'm now regretting because it's awkward to carry. I put my headphones on and press play on a Christmas playlist I made years ago. My

palms are starting to sweat despite the cold weather. I can't shake off this nervous feeling swirling around in my gut. Not even "Fairytale of New York," the greatest Christmas song of all time, can calm me. I'm not sure I can do this. I tell myself it's a mistake. If I get there and Jason's not there, I will give Mum and Dad their present, make an excuse, and go. Why did I think this was a good idea? It's around 10 o'clock when I get to the house. I only see Dad's car in the driveway, but that means nothing because I have no idea how my brother gets around. I walk in and prepare myself for the worst. Dad is in his armchair watching Oliver. I wish him a Merry Christmas and walk through to the kitchen. Mum has already started the dinner preparations. She sees me and wipes her hand on a tea towel.
"Merry Christmas, darling," she says, kissing me on the cheek.
"Where do you want me to put your present?" I ask her. "Stick it on the table, yours is in the living room, but we will do presents when your brother gets here." The mention of his name sets my heart racing, especially now that my plan has gone out the window. I place it on the small table that occupies the kitchen. It will be fine I tell myself, 10 years is a long time to heal old wounds, and who knows, he might have changed. All I know about him, from what Dad has told me, is that he's had more girlfriends than jobs, which isn't hard because he's only had about 2 of those. And his new girlfriend has got very wealthy parents. Like ridiculously wealthy. Which makes me think he might be less resentful if he's surrounded by money. I need to stop thinking about it because it's making me anxious, so I open the fridge in search of a drink. There's a litre bottle of Bailey's. I help myself to a large glass and join Dad in the living room. He's still watching the TV, and Fagin is showing Oliver how to pickpocket. Mum comes through and sits for a bit; she already looks knackered.
Now she knows how I've felt for the last few years when we've had them over for Christmas. We sit and watch the rest of Oliver, and when the credits roll, it's gone midday. Mum goes back to cooking,

and I start to think that maybe my brother's not coming. Dad and I are chatting about golf when I hear a car pull up outside. My heart is like a greyhound chasing after a rabbit. I hear my brother's voice as he walks up the driveway. He must have brought his girlfriend with him. He walks through the door and into the living room. And there he is, my brother. I get a good look at him, and he's aged terribly. His skin tone looks off, and his hair looks damaged and washed out from all the drugs. He smiles and I count more than one fake tooth where his teeth have rotted away. And he's skinny. I know I'm skinny, but he makes me look fat. But surprisingly, it hasn't made him ugly. One thing I can say about Jason growing up is that he was always good-looking, which is probably why he's always had girlfriends. That and he can bullshit his way out of a paper bag. He sees me sitting there, and none of us know what to do or say, so we just nod.
"Good to see you, brother," he finally says.
"Good to see you too, Jason," I respond. He then remembers his girlfriend is with him.
"Oh yeah, this is Rebecca," he says, introducing her to all of us. She says hi and smiles to everyone, and I breathe a sigh of relief because he's more likely to behave with her here."I've got something to show you all. Come outside," he says excitedly. We follow him outside, and there, parked next to Dad's car, is a silver/grey old-fashioned car. "This," he says, like a salesman from a car dealership, "is a 1966 Ford Mustang." When the three of us don't share his excitement, he tells us that it's worth £75,000.
"How have you managed to afford this, Jason?" Mum says, absolutely gobsmacked. "It was a Christmas present from Rebecca's dad. He's got a huge collection of vintage cars," he replies. None of us can quite believe what we've heard, and there's an awkward silence for a few minutes. "Who wants a drink?" Mum says, breaking it. We go inside and Mum pours everybody a glass of Bucks Fizz, and we all clink glasses and say, "Merry Christmas." I start to relax a little, knowing that as long as Jason and I aren't left in a room alone

together, it should be okay. Mum seats all of us around the table; Dad's at the head, I'm to the right, and Rebecca is to the left. Jason is next to her, and Mum is next to me.

"So how's work, Rob? Mum tells me you're working on something big," Jason asks me as he spoons some mash onto his plate.

"Yeah, it's nearly finished. Shooting the advert in April out in Rome." As I say it, I think maybe it comes off too braggy, but there's not a lot I can do about it, so I follow it up with, "What about you?"

"I'm working for Rebecca's dad. He owns his own software company, and he's bringing me in from the ground up to hopefully one day help him run it."

"Very nice," I say, trying so hard not to sound sarcastic.

"My dad loves him," Rebecca adds. "He says he's got so many great ideas."

He must really love him to give him a £75,000 car, I want to say but obviously don't, and feel bitter for even thinking it. Mum tops everyone's glasses up with more Bucks Fizz, except for Rebecca's, who's told us she's driving them home later. We pull the crackers, put on the paper hats, and read the terrible jokes you get inside. And for a moment, we look like a normal family celebrating Christmas. I bite into a parsnip.

"These parsnips are lovely, Mum," I say and I really mean it.

"Remember those ones we had at the club last week, Rob?" Dad says, turning to me.

"They were rock solid, nearly broke my tooth on one," I reply. I look around and Jason has that look about him. It's the look he has when Dad and I share something he's not involved in and he can't bear it. Mum, who is going to have the difficult role of peacekeeper today, feels the tension. "What's everyone doing for New Year's Eve?" she asks.

"Me and Rebecca are going to her parents. They're having this massive party. It's a proper black tie event with waiters and a DJ and everything. What are you doing, Rob?" He asks me.

"Not sure yet, might not even bother," I reply, trying not to sound envious. Because the truth is, I'm not envious of Jason and I never have been. He can turn up in an expensive car with his rich girlfriend and talk to me till he's blue in the face about black-tie events, but it will never make him a decent human. Every day he has to look in the mirror and think about the things he's done and the people he's hurt, and that's something I don't have to do. Besides, most people aren't asking to be rich; they just want to be comfortable.

"Oh yeah, I keep forgetting you're not with Michelle anymore, are you?" A small grin forms as he says it, and it's clear he's never once forgotten that fact. And then I realize Dad's comment about the golf club has struck a nerve. After we've eaten, Rebecca helps Mum with the dishes, and Dad, Jason, and I sit and make awkward small talk.

"Right, let's do presents," Mum says excitedly as they come back through to the living room. Mum and Dad open the slow cooker from me, and a £200 gift voucher to a very hard-to-get-into restaurant from Jason and Rebecca. Me and Jason are both given a card with £50 inside, and Jason gets a jumper. Then Dad hands me a present. As he does, I see the excitement on his face. I open it up, and it's a copy of "Remains of the Day" by Kazuo Ishiguro, and then I see it's a first edition. "Oh my god, Dad, this must have cost a fortune," I say, unable to contain myself.

"It was only £2.50," he says, laughing. "I went to a record fair, and a woman had a book stall there. Her husband left her for another woman, so she decided to sell all his books." Jason scoffs.

"Is there a problem, Jason?" Dad says, annoyed at his attempts to ruin the moment.

"No problem at all, just some things never change," he replies casually.

"What do you mean by that?" Dad demands.

"Rob gets something he's clearly always wanted and I get a jumper. It's like being kids again." I'm trying so hard not to snap.

"Time for pudding," Mum says. "Rob, come and give me a hand, please," she adds desperately. Once we get into the kitchen, I collar her. "I mean it, Mum," I say, when I'm sure no one can hear. "One more sarcastic comment or dig, and I'm leaving."

"Oh, Rob, stop being so sensitive. I told your father that giving you that book in front of your brother, was a bad idea. It was bound to rub him up the wrong way."

"Hang on a minute. You're fine with him parading his expensive car in front of all of us, but Dad's not allowed to give me a book he paid £2.50 for because he gets jealous."

"You know what your brother's like," is all she can say.

"Yeah, I do, and by the looks of things, he hasn't changed at all. He still only cares about things that are either for him or about him." I snap.

"He asked you about your job," she snaps back,

"Yeah, only so he could tell me he's working for a big software company."

"Please, Rob, just ignore him, and let's have a good day," she begs. We go back into the living room with a trifle and five bowls, and everybody's quiet while we eat. Dad turns on the TV, and "The Muppets Christmas Carol" is on. And I absolutely love this film; it is one of the best Christmas films. Bob Cratchit is asking Scrooge if they can have some more coal on the fire.

"I hate this film," Jason slurs, and I wonder how many drinks he's actually had. I look at him properly, and he looks worse for wear. Mind you I need to slow down because one thing I've learnt about alcohol. If you've got a chip on your shoulder the more you drink the bigger it gets. "Tiny Tim is just unbearable," he adds, almost yelling. As the film continues, he helps himself to more drinks. I think Dad might say something, but he doesn't. By the end of the film, Scrooge unlike Jason, has seen the error of his ways and he's bought the biggest turkey for them all to share, and everyone's singing as they walk to Bob Cratchit's house. "And now they're all friends, look, PATHETIC!" Jason shouts either to us or at the TV. No one's really sure.

"Jason, calm down. It's only a film," Rebecca is saying.

He scowls at her. "Let's have a game of charades, like we used to when we were kids," he says, standing up.

"Are you playing, Rob?"

"No I'm alright," I reply.

"God, you're so fucking boring. No wonder Michelle left you. How she stuck it out for all those years is beyond me." And that's it. He's got me, like a fish on a hook. He's reeled me in.

"Coming from the bloke who can't maintain a relationship for more than 5 minutes. And everything he touches turns to shit." I snap back.

"Oh perfect Rob, never made a mistake in his life, Mum and Dad's little golden boy. Mr. University, Mr. Bachelor's degree, Mr. Sun shines out of his fucking arse."

"There's a difference between a few little mistakes and totally fucking up your life. And I'm not going to apologize or feel guilty for doing well." I argue back.

"Apologize for doing well," he snarls. "There you go again, look, thinking you're better than everyone else. Like when we were kids and everything just got handed to you, while some of us struggled. Mum and Dad always helped you while I got shafted."

"They tried to help you out, but you weren't interested, Jason. You were too busy fucking about and getting brought home in police cars. And do you know what I never once heard you say? Sorry mum, sorry dad. Because nothing was ever your fault. Can you imagine what it was like for them to sit there night after night, not having a clue where you were or what you were doing? That any moment there could be a knock at the door and it's the police again."

"Pack it in, both of you," Mum shouts.

"It's fine, mum. Let him say what he didn't have the guts to say 10 years ago. Besides, look at how things turned out. I've got a great job at a massive company and a wonderful girlfriend," he says, turning and smiling at Rebecca. There's that bullshit I talked about. "And you are still making knockoff aftershave, living in a house on your own because your girlfriend realized that you were that boring. She had to fuck off out of the country just to get away from you."

"Jason, you're nothing but a sponge. You've sponged off Mum and Dad all your life, and now you're sponging off your girlfriend. And it won't be long until she sees through your bullshit, and you'll have to sell your car to fuel your drug habit."

He flies towards me and pins me up against the door, just like all those years ago, except this time Mum and Dad witness it, and he doesn't have a knife.

"Where's your knife?" I whisper through gritted teeth, soft enough that only he can hear. He doesn't have time to react because Dad grabs him by the scruff of his neck and pulls him off me. There's a moment of silence.

"Everyone's had a lot to drink. Rebecca, will you come and help me make coffee?" Mum asks. Rebecca, who is desperate to get away from the chaos, follows Mum into the kitchen. Dad turns to Jason and grits his teeth, "Apologize to your brother now."

"I knew you'd take his side, you always do. I'm not apologizing."

"If you don't apologize, then you're not welcome here anymore. I mean it, Jason."

"Mum would never let that happen," he replies smugly.

"She would if I told her I had to dispose of a knife that you'd earlier threatened your brother with," Dad fired back.

"Tell her, I don't care, I'm done with you all anyway." Mum and Rebecca come back through from the kitchen.

"Get your coat, Rebecca, we're leaving." I see the look of relief on her face as she goes to get her coat. We hear the car start up and they're gone. I sit down and start to drink my coffee, but the atmosphere is too tense. I get my coat and leave too.

14. Turning 30

January 2025

For the next few days, I replay the events of Christmas Day in my head. I'm so pissed off with myself for letting Jason get the best of me. But at the same time, I'm pleased that I got it off my chest because now everybody has some clarity and know where they stand.

I spend new years eve on my own, after what happened at christmas, I've decided to stop drinking for a bit and the thought of celebrating what has been a dreadful year doesn't fill me with much joy. I also purchased a proper pair of running trainers and started running again. This is, in no way, a New Year's resolution. I don't believe in that "new year, new me" bollocks, where people give up drinking, buy a gym membership, go for 2 weeks, and then never go again. I make myself a motivational playlist to run to.

Underworld – Born Slippy

New Order – Blue Monday

Faithless – Insomnia

Energy 52 – Cafe Del Mar

That kind of thing. I have to say, I've missed it. There's something so therapeutic about putting on some headphones, blocking out the world, and just running. The first couple of times, my legs feel like they are on fire. But it doesn't take me long to get back into the swing of things. It's my birthday on the 25th of January, the big three 0, and I decide that's when I'll have a drink, nothing mental, just a quiet one. Paul and Andy keep telling me I have to go all out because I'm only 30 once, and I keep reminding them that you're only every age once. January is such a blue month, you've still got the hangover of Christmas, and you spend most of the month evaluating whether or not your life is where you want it to be. Don't get me wrong, I've got things to look forward to. April isn't far away, and I'm looking forward to working on the advert and seeing Tiffany again, but Paul's moved in with Shelly, and Andy has started seeing someone, so I don't see them as much, and I feel as if I'm going nowhere on the relationship front.

I wake up on my birthday feeling the lowest I've felt in a long time. Birthdays are supposed to be happy, that's why people wish you a happy birthday. The clue's in the title. But 30 hits differently. It's the realization I'm no longer in my 20s and I'm alone. I've been kidding myself for nearly a year. I've told myself over and over again that I don't miss Michelle and that I'm better off without her. But the truth is I do miss her. I missed her a lot on Christmas Day, and I miss her even more today. And I hate her for leaving me. We spent our 18th together and our 21st. We were supposed to spend our 30th together, and our 40th and 50th, leaning on each other through middle age. And then, when we were in our 70s, and we were all burnt out and our bodies refused to work. We were going to retire and move to Spain, lie on the beach, and drink cocktails. This is the loneliest I've ever felt. But I have to push these feelings down because it's hard for a man to voice these feelings out loud, there's a reason for that and it comes from a deep lying fear. A fear that the words will be met with a mixture of mockery, feind interest and embarrassment, Especially when talking to other men. Men feel that if they tell another man exactly how they feel it will be met with a eye roll or a wave of awkwardness. When in reality most men would be willing to open up if they knew the other person would also. If only there was some code like a facial expression or a handshake to say it's ok you can talk to me because I know exactly how your feeling I've been there myself or I'm currently going through the same thing. I checked my phone and there were birthday wishes from Mum, Dad, Paul, and Andy. I don't have one from Michelle, and I'm not expecting one either. I also haven't received one from Tiffany, but I'm not sure if she knows it's my birthday, so she gets a pass. I try to lift my mood by going for a run, and it works until I get back home, and then I'm back to square one. I have no idea what to do today. All I know is that I'm going to Mum and Dad's tonight for dinner. Mum's making homemade chili, and then I've told Paul and Andy I'd go for a few drinks with them, so there's that to look forward to. I spend most of the day sitting on the sofa, watching old episodes of Friends.

I nip to the shop and get 2 bottles of red wine before getting the tube to Mum and Dad's. It's a bitterly cold night. You can smell it in the air. I walk up the driveway, walk through the door, and into the living room. I hear people, completely out of sync with each other, shout "surprise". There's Mum, Dad, Andy, Paul, and Shelly. As much as I appreciate the gesture, I can't help thinking that this is the lowest number of people I've ever seen at a party, and it's not like more people are on the way. But the really sad truth is that there are 5 people here; 2 of them are my parents, 2 of them I've only known a year and I met at work, and the other one is one of their girlfriends. I give everyone my best certificate smile and give my Mum a hug. I'm lonely, but I'm not ungrateful. I pour myself a drink and chat with Andy, Paul, and Shelly. Mum's put on a big buffet, and I help myself to a plate of cocktail sausages, mini quiches, cheese on a stick, that kind of thing. Dad's in charge of the music, and he's in his elements. I catch him smiling to himself every time someone moves along to one of his choices. After an hour or so, Mum tells him to turn the volume down and clinks a spoon against her glass to get everyone's attention.
"Thank you all for coming to Rob's 30th get-together," she says, and even she thinks it's too small to call it a party. "We are so proud of the man you've become, and we love you so much. Graham, come and say something nice about your son."

Dad walks over and stands next to Mum. "I can't believe I've got a 30-year-old son," he smiles.

"Rob, don't worry about turning 30. It's like my dad used to say, 30 is the new 20. Great bloke, terrible driver." Everybody laughs, except Mum.

"Your dad never used to say that," she scowls.

"It was a joke, Mary. Anyway, we are proud of you, son. Happy birthday." Mum sits me down and gives me a pile of presents. There's a suitcase, a Europe to UK plug adapter, a passport holder from Mum and Dad, and a travel pillow from Andy, Paul, and Shelly. I thank everyone for the presents, and the party resumes. I have to admit, it's just what I needed, and everyone seems to be enjoying themselves. I talk to mum and Shelly in the living room about Rome and the things I'd like to see when I get out there, while Dad, Paul, and Andy are in the kitchen. I go through to get a drink, and they're not in there. I hear voices coming from outside, so I go see where they've gone. I walk into the garage to find the three of them deep in conversation about the best Cure album.

"Your dad is so cool," Paul says to me smiling, "Look at this record collection, it's like HMV in here." I laugh and join the conversation. It nearly gets heated when Andy tries telling my dad that Wish is better than Disintegration. When my dad starts yawning, I say it's getting late and think we should call it a night. We say our goodbyes to my parents and get on the tube. When it's just me left on the tube, I reflect on what turned out to be a good 30th birthday. I get home, turn the TV on, and flick through the channels. Around 11:30, my phone vibrates. It's a message from Tiffany. It reads:

"Happy belated birthday, Rob. Hope you've had a good one x."

I smile to myself. She didn't forget.

15. First time flyer.

Friday the 25th of April 2025.

3 months later.

I can imagine packing to be stressful at the best of times, but when you don't know how long you're going to be going for, it's got to be 10 times harder. I've checked the weather and it's 18°C in Rome at the minute. So I need to pack for warm weather. I'm actually starting to get really nervous. I've never been on a plane before. I've been to France with Mum and Dad as a kid, but we took the ferry. I didn't realize how stressful it is to go abroad. I had to do my passport photos twice because I accidentally smiled in the first set. I had to get travel insurance, I bought a travel money card to convert pounds into euros, and I spent countless hours Googling what to do at the airport. Mum printed me off a checklist, and I'm going through it. So far, I've packed.

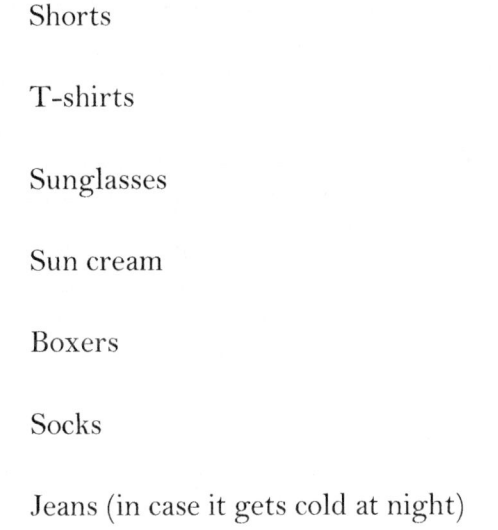

Shorts

T-shirts

Sunglasses

Sun cream

Boxers

Socks

Jeans (in case it gets cold at night)

Our flight is at 10:00 am from Heathrow, which is where I'm meeting Paul and Andy. I've got to take the tube from King's Cross to Paddington, which takes 11 minutes. Then a train from Paddington to Heathrow, which takes 30 minutes. After factoring in that I've got to be there 2 hours before my flight (which just adds to the stress), I need to leave the house no later than 7:00 am. From my hours of googling airport rules and regulations, I found out that you can't take liquids of a certain height. So I've bought a load of travel-sized shampoos and deodorants and packed them with the rest of my stuff. I even packed a box of 40 tea bags just in case the ones in Italy are shit. Tiffany was right; I am ridiculously British. When I finish packing, I watch a bit of TV and call it a night. Excitement, nerves, and anticipation fight for my attention, and I struggle to sleep.

I wake up 10 minutes before the 6 o'clock alarm but refuse to get up until it goes off. I shower, brush my teeth, and make myself a cup of tea. It's too early to eat; I'll get something at King's Cross. I zip up my suitcase, put my passport in the rucksack I'm taking as hand luggage, and leave the house. The sound of my suitcase wheels scraping across the pavement as I make my way to King's Cross. There's a slight chill in the air, and despite it being early, King's Cross is already quite busy. There's a man and a woman in fluorescent orange fleeces, setting up a stall to try and tempt people into getting car insurance. Personally, I wouldn't have picked outside the tube as the location for it, considering most people are getting on the tube because they don't own a car. There's a smell of warm cookies coming from one of the many food stalls; it makes my stomach grumble. And the bloke who thinks he's Jesus is having a full-blown conversation with a pigeon about how he should have bought Apple shares when he had the chance. I manage to avoid the insurance salespeople and make my way inside.
  I get a pain au chocolate and a cup of tea to go before going back outside and down the stairs to the platforms. Getting on the tube

with a suitcase is a traumatic experience; it's fucking awkward. Luckily, it's not rush hour, and I'm only on here for 11 minutes, but I'm pressed up against the pole, and every time the tube rocks, I have to stop it from rolling off and smashing into people's shins. I get off at Paddington and head straight for the train, and I'm thankful it is a train and not a tube because it means I can put my luggage in the holder and relax for a bit. I put my headphones in, but instead of listening to music, I put on an app that translates English phrases into Italian ones. I've been listening to it for the last few days in order to impress Tiffany by speaking a bit of the lingo. It's not exactly Colin Firth in Love Actually, but it's something. But once again, here lies the problem I've got. For months, I've thought of Tiffany, but only as a passing thought because I wasn't seeing her every day. Yet, the week before the trip, all the strong feelings I have for her are reiterated. It's like Pandora's box is open, and lust, desire, and admiration all blend together to make some sort of lovesick cocktail. The only way this is ever going to end is when the project is over, and we go our separate ways. Or she leaves her husband and falls in love with me. But I've got more chance of being crowned world's strongest man than that ever happening. I get off at Heathrow station and have to take a lift to the upper level. When it gets to the top, the doors slide open, and there is Heathrow Airport standing before me. The terminals are clearly marked in massive letters, so it couldn't be any easier. There's a smoking area tucked away in the far corner, and I see Paul and Andy chatting away while Paul vapes. I wheel my suitcase over to them, and they spot me.

"Are you ready for the lads' holiday?" Paul says.

"I remember my first lad's holiday. I took a packet of 12 condoms, and I think I came back with 13," Andy laughs. I want to say that it's three blokes (one of which has a girlfriend) going to Italy on business; it's hardly Kevin and Perry Go Large. But instead, I say, "Ready as I'll ever be. What are you looking forward to the most?"

I ask them. Paul says the "Colosseum", and Andy says "eating pizza for breakfast, lunch, and dinner." We go inside, and the place is like a maze; there are so many check-in desks. We find the one we are supposed to be at and join the queue. The woman behind the counter asks for our passports and tickets and tells us to put our luggage on the conveyor belt to be weighed, before handing us our boarding passes. We then make our way to security and go through the metal detectors, and for some reason, my heart is racing, and I have no idea why, especially when they ask me to take my shoes off. I've not got anything on me that I shouldn't have, but the whole concept is so nerve-racking. Once security is happy that I'm not a drug smuggler or a terrorist, I am allowed to go through. When we reach the other side, we hit duty-free. They've got a wide range of aftershaves from Gucci to Moncler. I feel a stab of excitement at the thought of ours being alongside these top brands one day. After 15 minutes of browsing, I'm bored.
"What's next?" I say to Andy.
"That's it until we board," he replies.
"What do you mean, 'that's it'? We still have an hour until we fly. Why the fuck did we have to be here 2 hours before?"
"Don't worry," he laughs at my outburst, "Because we won't be getting an inflight meal, we can go get breakfast and a pint at the bar."
"A pint? It's 9 o'clock in the morning."
"That doesn't matter in an airport, mate," he replies. And he's right. I look at the bar, and it's full of holidaymakers sitting cradling half-empty pint glasses of beer. Some are even taking pictures of it, which I'm guessing is for some Social media platform or some bollocks like that—#holiday #lookatme. I get a full English with everything, but I can't drink a pint that early, so I get a cup of tea instead. I can't believe we still have an hour. I feel like Tom Hanks in the film The Terminal. Time just seems to stand still. "I've got an idea for a new game show," Paul says, breaking the silence.

"Instead of Blind Date, it's called Blind Skate. Contestants are blindfolded and have to skate through an obstacle course."

"Yeah, that doesn't sound dangerous at all," Andy says, laughing.

When it's finally time to board, we make the long walk to Gate 30. We watch the upper-class people board first, and then we are allowed on. We walk through the jet bridge to the plane and get stopped by the stewardess, who asks to see our tickets. She points right – for Economy – and I look for seat 24A. When we get to the three seats that make up our row, Andy asks me if I want to sit next to the window because I've never flown before, and I say yes. I climb across the first 2 seats and settle in next to the window. I'm mesmerized by the fact that there are charging ports for your phone and that you can pay for WiFi. The cabin crew goes through the safety instructions and before I know it, we are ready to go. My heart jumps when we start to move and I see the airport slowly passing us by. Then the plane stops, and I think there's something wrong. Then we accelerate and gradually pick up more and more speed. Then I'm thrown back and the plane slants. I look out the window, and we are rising and rising, and all I can see are small specks of buildings and grass that we've left behind. It's scary and exhilarating at the same time. Then the plane rights itself, and there's the popping of the ears I've heard so much about. The pilot turns the seatbelt sign off, and everyone unclips their seatbelts, so I do too. Most people, including Paul and Andy, occupy themselves with either a book or some music, but I'm just taking it all in. I can't stop looking out the window at the clouds; they just don't look real. After about an hour, the novelty wears off, so I put my headphones in and listen to some more translations.

All of a sudden, the plane drops a little, and I hear the rattling of the trays as the aircraft sways side to side, and my chair starts to shake. Well, this is just fucking brilliant, I think to myself. It's my first time flying, and it's going to result in death. It's like a scene from a film where any minute the plane has a mechanical fault and starts to deteriorate. The tail detaches itself from the rest of the plane, and the whole thing goes down. I look across to Paul and Andy. Andy is sitting there with music on, looking really peaceful. Paul is casually reading. Why are they not panicking? I look at the rest of the passengers and everyone seems relaxed and normal. Am I the only one who can feel this? The plane drops again and my heart drops with it. I take a big deep breath, and then it's over. I've survived it.

"Did none of you feel that?" I say to both of them.

"What, that bit of turbulence? Yeah, that's normal," Paul says.

"That was turbulence?" I almost yell.

"Why did you think it was bad?"Andy laughs.

"It was horrible. I think my heart fell out of my arse," I reply. I relax for the rest of the flight, safe in the knowledge that the cabin crew aren't just there for show. They actually know what they are doing. The plane touches down on Italian soil and we vacate the plane. We play the game of trying to get our luggage off the revolving conveyor belt before it goes back around again. It's like one of those sushi restaurants where you choose your own food as it comes around. Our luggage comes out and we pull it off. By the exit, there's a cluster of drivers holding signs with people's names on them, like the Robinson family, the Jone's, John's stag Do. I see one that says Amato's and thinks that's got to be ours. Our hotel is an hour away. The driver takes us right up to the front of the hotel. It's a massive historic-looking building. It almost looks like a Renaissance painting. It overlooks a huge garden with stone pillars that look perfect for an outside wedding. We walk up to reception, which is sitting on big slabs of mosaic tiles. We get checked in, drop our luggage off at the rooms, and explore the rest of the hotel. It's a very business-oriented hotel, full of conference rooms and a big lecture hall. Once we've run out of places to see, we have no idea what to do or where to go, so we eat at the hotel and have a few drinks before calling it a night.

16. Rome

Saturday 26th of April 2025

The following morning, I go down for breakfast. The room is set out with tables scattered around the edges and one long display buffet table in the middle, with food on both sides. It's a continental breakfast of cereal, pastries, and fruit. I help myself to a cannoli, some fruit, and a cup of tea. I spot Andy and Paul at a table in the corner and go and join them. "What the hell have you got there?" I say to Andy, sitting down. "Breakfast cake," he replies with a mouthful of sponge. "Cake for breakfast, is that even a thing?" "It is here," he answers, happily munching away. "By the way," Paul begins, "does anyone even know we're here?"
"That's a good point," I say, biting into a strawberry. "I'll message Tiffany." As I say this, I catch Paul and Andy sharing a little smile. I send her a message, saying that we are at the hotel, having breakfast, and we are not sure what to do. She sends me one back which reads,

"Oh good you're here, I was starting to worry you weren't coming. I take it they didn't give you your welcome pack at reception? Anyway, it's all in there, see you soon x."

We finish eating breakfast and go to get the packs from reception. It's not really a welcome pack, it's more of an envelope. I read the letter.

Rob,

We hope your stay is a pleasant one. Attached to this letter is a 7-day metro pass that will get you around the city. The nearest metro station is Cornelia, take the metro to Spagna. Tiffany will meet you there and explain the rest.

Welcome to Rome.

After slipping the metro card into my wallet, we ask the concierge which way the metro station is, and he tells us to head out of the hotel grounds and turn right. It's a 10-minute walk to the station, and we can't miss the metro sign. On the way, I take in Rome. It's exactly the way I imagined it to be: busy, vibrant, men in suits riding Lambretta's to work, restaurants, bistros, coffee shops on every street corner, jam-packed with people outside drinking espressos. We keep walking until we see an "M" sign for the metro. I brace myself for what I think is going to be all the chaos of the London Underground but in a different country. However, as we walk down the stairs, it couldn't be further away from that. There are no stampedes, no staying to the right, and no 100mph commuters. It's so mellow. It's like the London Underground has taken a hot lavender bath, lit a candle, and put some Marvin Gaye on. I looked at the board, and there are only 2 lines: Line A and Line B, which cover 73 stations, as opposed to London's 11 lines covering 272 stations. The Cornelia station is on Line A, and the station we want, Spagna, is also on A. It takes 13 minutes, and that's pretty much all there is to it. We get on the metro and move through the stations until we reach ours. We get off and walk the short distance out of the station. It's just gone 10 o'clock, it's 21°C, the sun is beaming, and it's gorgeous. The exit to the station leads to an alleyway of shops and lots of outdoor stalls selling handmade jewellery and street art. We get out into the open, and there's Tiffany sitting on a wall between two palm trees. She's wearing a floral blue and white dress, a pair of designer sunglasses, and some suede-coloured sandals. The warm weather really suits her; she looks as attractive as ever. She smiles when she sees us. "Are you ready to see Rome? I'm Tiffany, and I will be your tour guide," she says. She takes us to the left, alongside a swarm of fellow tourists. And then slightly to the right. we reach a street called Via

Condotti, which is full of high-end fashion shops like Gucci, Versace, Missoni, Fendi, Prada, Armani, and Valentino. Jewellers such as Bulgari, Cartier, and Rolex. They all have security guards at their doors, and a tie from any of them probably costs a month's wages. So we don't actually go into any of them. Once we finish walking down the street of the unaffordable shops, she takes us back up to the foot of the famous Spanish Steps. It is already filled with tourists sitting and basking in the sun. The area is split into 3 sections. There is space on the left side, so we climb up, sit for a bit, and take in the view.

"Did you have a nice Christmas?" she asks.

"Yeah, very quiet, very uneventful," I reply, which couldn't be further from the truth.

"What about you?" I ask.

"Same really," she replies, brushing her hair away from her sunglasses.

"What do you have planned for us today then?" Andy says excitedly.

"I'm taking you to the Colosseum, Roman Forum, and then to Palatine Hill to see the ruins, but there's an ice cream parlour I want to take you to first." We take the steps to the bottom and head back towards the metro station.

"Is it that one there with the queue so big it's out the door?" Paul asks disgruntledly.

"Yeah, but I promise you it's worth it," she smiles. When we finally get in, there are 150 ice cream flavours to choose from. There's a whole section just for chocolate. There's hazelnut chocolate, orange chocolate, whiskey chocolate, coconut chocolate, Ferrero Rocher. There's pistachio, mango, kiwi, and melon. There's Mars, Snickers, and Oreo. "OH MY GOD," shouts Paul, "there's a Viagra flavour."

"I've not had it, but apparently it tastes like champagne and it has 25mg of Viagra in it," Tiffany says, laughing.

"Are you going to try it, Paul?" Andy says, egging him on.

"No, because I'm afraid it's going to work, and I really don't want to walk around the Colosseum with a hard-on." We each pick our flavours, and I've gone for lemon cake. It's so nice and refreshing. Once we've finished our ice creams, we jump back on the metro and change to the B line. The station we want is called Colosseo, which makes sense for the Colosseum. Tiffany tells us it only takes 15 minutes.

"So, how far is the Colosseum from the station then?" I ask.

"Oh, you will see," is all she says. And we do see because as we stop off and walk out of the station, the Colosseum almost hits you in the face. It's absolutely massive and so iconic. I get my phone out and take a few pictures, Andy and Paul do the same. We scan our tickets and go through the entrance. There's an elevator to the top, or you can walk up the steps. We choose to walk and instantly regret it. The stone steps are huge. By the time we got to the top, my legs hurt in places I didn't even know I had muscles. Luckily, I've been running twice a week; otherwise, I'd be completely screwed. The Colosseum is just as impressive inside as it is outside. Sitting around the amphitheater and looking down at the stage where the gladiators fought, you can feel the history. After a full afternoon of sightseeing, my stomach moans at me for not feeding it. Tiffany must have heard it because she says, "I think it's time for pizza." The next station we need is Termini, which is only 5 minutes away, so we are off as quickly as we got on. We walk down a few side streets to a place called "Rifugio Romano." I remember it's Tiffany's favourite restaurant, so of course, we were going to eat here. We get a table in the corner and take our seats. The waiter walks over and asks what he can get us. "Posso avere una pinta di peroni Per favore" I say, which is can I have a pint of peroni please in italian. Tiffany looks at me impressed.

I watch as the waiter takes an ice-cold tankard out of a large freezer and puts it under the Peroni tap. When he hands it to me, I take a sip, and it's so refreshing. "What pizza would you recommend?" I say to Tiffany.

"Oh, that's easy, Margherita."
"Really? Plain cheese and tomato?" I reply, shocked.
"Yeah, that's how pizza is supposed to be. You're supposed to be able to taste the actual pizza, not overcomplicate it with loads of toppings."
So, I order a Margherita on her say-so, and once again, she is right. I bite into the first slice, and the sweet, rich Italian tomato mixed with the stringy mozzarella cheese is mouth-watering. Every bite I take, I'm fully aware that this is probably the best pizza I'm ever going to taste. Tiffany smiles when she sees how much I'm enjoying it. We all order another drink and catch up on things like work and just life in general. Tiffany tells us she lives in a 2-bed apartment not far from the Termini train station. "Will we get to meet your husband then, Tiffany?" Andy asks curiously.
"No, I don't think so. He's working nights at the minute, so he sleeps most of the day," she replies, sipping her drink. As the night draws on and Rome really lights up, we decide to call it a night.
"I'm pleased you've all enjoyed today," Tiffany begins. "Tomorrow we need to start looking for a street to shoot this advert. Mr. Amato wants to get the film crew and actors in as soon as possible, so we need to get our heads together. Anyway, have a nice night, the three of you." She adds, and we all watch her leave.

The next few days are spent looking for a side street that we can use for the advert. We need one that's got just the right amount of coffee shops and restaurants, so that when we put the extras in they don't look out of place. On Wednesday, we find the perfect one. It's got the Vatican just visible in the background, which will look amazing on camera. We had to get permission but it's all fine. That's the good news, the bad news is, we are no longer needed. Despite what our boss Steve said about us being here to watch the advert being shot, it turns out we're not going to be. Which is a massive kick in the teeth, especially since it was all our hard work that got us here. We are told thank you for everything and that our flight back to London will be on Friday, so we've only got 2 days left, which is a bit of a bummer. Determined to make the most of the time we have left, we are going to try and cram in as much as we can, which is going to be a lot easier now that we've stopped looking for a spot to shoot the advert.

Thursday morning, we are showered and have breakfast by 9:00 a.m. By 9:30 a.m., we're on our way to meet Tiffany at the San Luigi Dei Francesi Church to see some Caravaggio paintings. I'm so pleased that even though the project is as good as done, she's still spending the next two days with us. But it's like she says, with her husband working nights, she will only be sitting at home anyway, trying not to wake him, so there's not a lot else she can do. After lunch, we go to Villa Borghese Park and rent Segways. As the day draws on and it starts to get dark, Tiffany takes us to her favourite place, the Trevi Fountain. In the middle of the fountain is a large shell above two horses, ridden by Tritons, with water flowing around them, and it looks stunning all lit up. We go down to the fountain and toss a coin in, which apparently ensures our return to Rome. I get the sense that Tiffany isn't her usual self today; she's been subdued all day and I can't work out why. When it's time for dinner, she tells us she's not feeling very well and that she's going to call it a day. I'm devastated because my time with her is coming to an end, and I'm not ready for it to be. Tomorrow could be the last time I ever see her, and the thought of that is more than I can bear. In fitting with our attempt to squeeze in as much of Rome as we can, after dinner, we stay out and have a few drinks in the bars close to the fountain. I have no idea how it happens. The three of us are walking back to the metro station; it's 12;45 am. We stop at a street stall selling pictures of the Colosseum, done in spray paint. I look around and I can't see Andy and Paul. I tell myself it's fine; I know where the station is. I've walked past it so many times tonight. As I make my way in that direction, I have to walk past the Trevi Fountain again. I realize there's nobody down there; I've got it all to myself. I've got to go down and get a picture of it like this before I go. I make my way down, stand in front of the fountain, and get a great landscape picture of it. As I'm putting my phone in my pocket, I hear a voice. "Told you it was amazing, didn't I?" I whip my head around and see Tiffany tucked in the corner on her own.

"Hello," I shout, a little too excitedly and feel a bit embarrassed for doing so.

"What are you doing here?" I ask.

"I couldn't sleep; the house is just so empty. I hate it, and when I can't sleep, I come here." She replies. I sit down next to her.

"How are you feeling?" I ask.

"I'm fine, I was never poorly." I look at her confused. Before I can ask she explains. "as tomorrow is our last day together I may as well tell you my story." I sit on the stone seat with my back against the wall and listen. And she begins. "I'm originally from Bristol. Me and my mum moved to London when I was 16. I never knew my dad he was a one-night thing and never wanted anything to do with me. I did well at school and college but not well enough to get a scholarship and there was no way Mum could afford to send me to university. When I turned 22 my mum died in a car crash, she was only 52. I worked as much as I could to keep a shitty one-bed apartment, but I was struggling. I decided to go to night school at the university to try and get a degree. I chose Marketing and English Literature. The professor who taught the English Literature class was the famous author Frank Gold. I can tell by the look on your face that you've heard of him." I nod. "Well, Frank had a gaggle of girls who would fawn over him. They would approach him after lectures and tell him how much they enjoyed his class, as well as how great he was. I wasn't one of those girls, which is why I think he took a liking to me. He pursued me, and I let him. He was famous and very attractive. We started going out in secret, which wasn't that hard since he had a place off campus. One night, he invited me and a few other students so it wouldn't look suspicious, to a get-together at his house with three other famous authors. Midway through the get-together, a few of us were talking in a circle. It was me, another student, Frank, and another author. The other author made a joke at Frank's expense, and I laughed. I was a little bit drunk. I hung back after everyone had gone because I was staying at Frank's. He confronted me about laughing at him, and I nervously laughed again. And that's when he hit me. He pulled back his fist and punched me in the face. It was so hard that he broke my nose."

I look at her sympathetically. "Now I know what you're thinking. I can see the look on your face. You think it's a typical story where the guy apologizes profusely, promises to never do it again, the girl forgives him, and he does it again like they always do. That wasn't the case, I was gone. I quit his class and focused all my efforts on getting a degree in marketing. Which I managed to do. After that, I thought, that was it, but he kept showing up at my house saying he missed me and wanted me back. I saw an advert for a job at Amato's out here and went for it. With Mum gone, there was nothing keeping me there. So when I got the job, I packed up and left."

"And that's when you met your husband," I say when she finishes. She just nods.

"Today is the anniversary of my mum's death, so that's why I've been a bit off today. I'm sorry." I want to put my arm around her, but I don't.

"Don't be silly, you have nothing to be sorry for."

"Okay, well, you've heard my story, what's yours?" she says, wiping a tear from her right cheek. I tell her everything, even the stuff about my brother. when I finish, she looks at me the same way I looked at her – with a 'sorry that happened to you' kind of look. For a moment, there's a calm silence between us. And then we hear footsteps. A young couple descends the steps to the fountain. We stay silent and they don't spot us.

"Beautiful, isn't it?" the young lad says to his girlfriend before getting down on one knee and asking her to marry him.

She sobs and says "yes". They spend the next couple of minutes enjoying the moment. They are so caught up in it that they still don't see us.

When they leave, I look at Tiffany. "I've got an idea," I say. She looks at me skeptically. "What about, instead of the advertisement being a man confidently walking to a job interview, we go in a completely different direction altogether?"

"Like what?" she looks at me like I've lost my mind.

The advert starts with a young lad, someone nervous-looking, like Dylan North, the lad who played that kid who got bullied in that BBC drama. Do you know who I mean? "Yeah, I do. He's really good and really popular at the minute," she replies.

"So, it starts with, let's say, him. He's getting ready for a date with his girlfriend, but it's not a normal date. He's going to propose to her. He uses the aftershave. The advert cuts to the date; he gets down on one knee, and she says yes. The advert then jumps to their wedding day. He's in his suit, about to get married. Once again, he uses the aftershave before walking down the aisle. The message it sends out is that everyone needs an aftershave for a special occasion, and ours is that aftershave. What do you think?" "I think it's fucking brilliant, Rob."

"Really?" I say, getting excited.

"Hang on, how about we go that one step further? The advert jumps again to years in the future, and he's giving his son the aftershave for Christmas. You know, like a heartfelt John Lewis type of advert."

"That's even better," I reply. We both look at each other with pure excitement. Our faces are 5 inches apart. My heart is beating out of my chest. I think she's going to kiss me, but she doesn't, and after 30 seconds, the moment seems to have passed, and we both back away a little bit.

"What if it's too late?" I say, dejected. 'Hasn't the advert been approved?'

"Yeah, it's been approved. But it's not scheduled to be shot for another month," she replies, sounding optimistic. "Anyway, we will find out tomorrow, won't we?" she adds.
"How will we find out tomorrow?" I ask.
"Because tomorrow morning, I'm going to Mr. Amato to pitch the idea."

17. When It Rains, It Pours.

Friday, 2nd May 2025

The next morning, I fill Paul and Andy in on the events of last night, leaving out the bits about Tiffany's past. They both think the advert is a great idea but aren't convinced Mr Amato will go for the new idea. By 10 o'clock, we haven't heard anything, so we get on the metro and go chill out by the Spanish Steps and try some more ice cream flavours. Around 1 o'clock, I get a text message from Tiffany asking me where we are. She meets us at a coffee shop. We try to read her face as she walks towards us. She takes a seat.
"Right, I don't even know where to start with this," She says, as she takes off her sunglasses.
"I've spoken to Luca, and he loves the idea, and he's fully on board." We are all waiting for the 'but.'
"After a few phone calls to various people, this is where we're at. They are willing to shoot the new advert. We have also spoken to Dylan North's agent, and he has agreed to do it." She sees the excitement on our faces, "but." "there's the 'but' we were all waiting for."
"He won't fly to Rome. He's just too busy. He's shooting a new drama in Manchester and can only squeeze in an hour here and there between filming. So, he has compromised and said if we shoot it in Manchester, he will do it, and his agent has promised he will make it happen. Luca loved our idea so much that he's given it the go-ahead." When she finishes, I look at her for any indication of what this means for her. And when she gives me nothing, I have to ask the question.
"What about you? Are you staying here?"
"And let you three take all the glory? No way. I'm coming to Manchester. I've already booked my flight," she says, smiling.
"Won't your husband mind?" Andy asks.
"When this opportunity came up, we sat down and talked it through. He told me to go for it, and said that I would regret it if I

didn't do it. Besides, it will be over soon and it's not like I'm moving to Manchester." That night, we celebrated with a nice meal and a few shots of limoncello. And sat around the Trevi Fountain one last time. By the end of the night, we said our goodbyes to Tiffany and went back to the hotel to pack our stuff, ready for our early morning flight. As we wheeled our suitcases out of the hotel the following morning, I got one last look at Rome before we headed home to London.

When I went away, I told my mum that I wasn't going to be back until 2:00 am Sunday morning because I knew she would be straight on the phone, asking me about the trip, and I really wanted a night just to relax. I settle on the sofa and scan the internet for takeaway places. I have to eat something that isn't pizza, lasagna, or spaghetti. In the end, I have a Chinese, sit back, and put a film on. It doesn't stop raining all night, a clear indication that I'm back home. I hold out for as long as I can, but about midway through the film, I can feel myself drifting, so I turn off the film and go to bed. I wake up to the sound of my phone vibrating across my bedside table. I check the caller ID, it says "Mum". I check the time, it's 6:30am. What is she doing calling me as early as this? I know I haven't spoken to her for a week, but this is ridiculous. "Hello, mum," I say, failing to suppress a yawn.

"Rob, I need you to come to the hospital. It's your dad, he's had a heart attack."

Suddenly, I'm awake. It's amazing how your body reacts to really bad news. It's like getting a big electric shock, it jolts you awake. I don't have time to mess about with the tube, so I order an Uber to Watford General Hospital. I put on any clothes I can find, grab my keys and my wallet, and wait outside. As I wait for the Uber, I'm constantly trying to get a hold of Mum to find out more, but she's not picking up. When the car arrives, I climb in the back. I start to

panic. So many things run through my mind. Is he okay? How severe is it? What caused it? I want answers. I try Mum again and get no joy. When the car pulls up to the hospital, I pay the driver and hurry into the hospital. I ask the receptionist where Graham Swan is, and she tells me he's in the CCU (Cardiac Care Unit). I follow the signs, and as I walk down the corridor, I spot Mum. She gets up out of a chair. Her face is stained with tears. I throw my arms around her and her face soaks the shoulder of my hoodie.
"What happened?" I ask.
"He got up in the middle of the night to go to the toilet and collapsed on the stairs," she replies.
"He's going to be alright though, isn't he?" I ask desperately.
"There's nothing they can do other than make him comfortable, Rob, and that's it," she replies, her voice wavering.
"What do you mean, that's it? It can't be it. It just can't be," I feel the warmth of a tear slide down my face.
"You need to go in and say your goodbyes. I'm going to try your brother again." That explains why I couldn't get hold of Mum; she can't get hold of Jason. Which is fucking Typical. I enter the room, and I see my dad. my hero. hooked up to machines. I almost walk out; it's too much to bear. I stand over him, and his eyes meet mine.
"Hello, son," he says, his voice strained. He asks me for some water. I get the little cup with the straw and hold it close to his mouth so he can drink it.
"Rob, listen to me," he begins.
"Michelle was right." I look at him, confused.
"I don't mean she was right to leave, that's not what I'm saying. But she was right about living your life. I've spent the last hour lying here, and do you know what I've thought about?" I shake my head. "My wedding day, the day you and your brother were born, birthdays, Christmases. "The look on your face when you got your first bike, and the determination to get back on when you fell off. Your brother's reaction when his feet first felt sand, the two of you making a sandcastle together and then both crying because the sea

swept it away. And do you know what I haven't thought about? I shake my head again. "Work, or how much it cost me to turn the garage into a music den, or how big the TV is in the living room. Because, in the end, those things don't matter. Life's about memories and finding things that make you happy, and doing those things every chance you get. What I'm saying is there's nothing bigger than the little things in life, and those little things are the things we will remember."
When he finishes and I take in everything he's said, I know he's right.
"Tell me about Rome," he says after a few minutes. So, I tell him, and he looks content for the first time since I got here. He smiles at certain bits of the stories, but he doesn't talk, and it's a sign that he's getting weaker. Halfway through telling him about the food, Mum comes back into the room.
"Jason's on his way," she says weakly. I step outside with her.
"You managed to get a hold of him then," I say, relieved.
"No, I still can't get a hold of him," she replies, drained. "But I thought you said he was on his way." Confusion fills my face. "I had to say that. How can I tell him that his son is not picking up his phone? I've left him a message after a message, and no one knows where he is."
"Let me try him," I say, trying to calm her. I ring 3 or 4 times, and it just keeps ringing. "Let me get you a cup of tea and a sandwich from the canteen. You keep trying him and I'll be back soon."
"I'm not hungry, Rob."
"You need to eat, Mum." I go to the canteen and get us both a cup of tea and a cheese and ham sandwich. When I get back, my mum is in the room with my dad. The doctor is in there with her. As I enter, I put the tea and sandwiches on the table. Mum turns to me with tears streaming down her face, "He's gone, Rob." She collapses into me, and we fall apart together. The doctor gives us a bit of time to sit with him, and when we are ready, he's taken away to be washed and taken to the morgue. We go back out into the corridor,

and Mum sits in the seat. The doors to the ward open, and Jason comes through. At first, I don't recognize him; he looks like he's put on weight. He's not fat, just filled out.

Mum stands up, "Where the hell have you been, Jason?" he goes to speak, but she interrupts him.

"I don't want to hear some bullshit excuse, I'm sick of it, we all are". I've never seen her this angry. "We've tried calling you and calling you, and you haven't picked up. We've left messages that you've just ignored. And now it's too late. Your dad's gone, and you never got to say goodbye." When Jason hears this, he breaks down.

"Wherever you were, I hope it was important. Where were you, Jason? Come on, tell me, come on."

"I WAS IN REHAB!" he yells.

"What?" Mum says, stunned. "Why were you in rehab?"

"Because I'm a drug addict, and I've fucked my life up, Mum, that's why," he sobs. "And I wanted you and Dad to be proud of me for once in my life. You're not allowed your phone; it's part of the rehabilitation process. The staff looks after them. I only found out about your calls and messages because my phone was going crazy. The staff member on shift thought it must be really important, which it obviously was, and gave me my phone back." His voice continues to break. "I came as soon as I could, but it turns out I'm too late. And now he's gone, and I never got a chance to say

goodbye." For the first time in my life, I feel sorry for him.

"Come on, let's drop mum off at home because she's knackered and needs sleep, and you and I will go for a coffee." I say. He nods, and the three of us leave the hospital. We get to the cafe, and Jason finds us a table. I go to the counter, order two cups of coffee, and bring them over to the table. He adds sugar and milk and takes a sip.

"I'm sorry, Rob," he says. They are the words I never in a million years thought I would hear from him. "I'm sorry for Christmas, I'm sorry for what happened the night before you went to university, and most of all I'm sorry for being a shitty brother." I'm speechless. A silence descends over us.

"I don't mean to be rude, but why now?" I finally say. He takes another sip of his coffee. "When I left at Christmas, I spent the next couple of days blaming you, like I always did. But then, when my birthday came around in February, I got a text message from Mum wishing me a happy birthday. But I never got one from Dad. And that hurt me. It hurt me so much, that I started using again. And well let's just say it completely fucked up my relationship with Rebecca. She told me she never wanted to see me again. So, I lost my job, And my girlfriend. She let me keep the car though," he chuckles lightly to himself.

"So, I checked into a rehab centre, and one thing you get in there is a lot of free time to think about the things you've done and reflect on the choices you've made. And one thing I realized, amongst other things, is how much of an arsehole I've been to you. And it was nothing but pure jealousy. Look, Rob, I'm not expecting you to forgive me. I just want you to know how sorry I am."

When he finishes, I look at him for a minute. "Are you hungry?" I say.

"Starving," he replies. I buy us both a full English breakfast, and we sit and talk about Dad. And it's probably the longest conversation I've ever had with him.

18. Tank Park Salute

I ask Steve if I could take a week's holiday so that I could help my mum with the funeral plans and other things around the house. And he tells me to have it as compassionate leave, which is really nice of him. Jason is going back to rehab (his idea) because he doesn't want to spiral and feels it's the best place for him. But he will be here for the funeral. Speaking of which, it's arranged for the 22nd of May, which is just over 2 weeks from now. I think it's a bit soon, but I suppose it's so the family of the deceased doesn't have it looming over them and it's easier to get closure.

My mum asks me if I can write the eulogy. And I tell her I will. She tells me that when talking about funerals, Dad specifically asked for his eulogy to have no mention of his job as a builder. He'd always said that the only people who should be defined by their jobs are those who actually enjoyed them or if their profession was something really cool like a musician, author, or astronaut – that sort of thing. Because for him, being a builder paid the bills, nothing more. She also asked me to choose two songs: one to come in to and one for when he goes into the cremation retort.

This is a lot harder than writing the eulogy. How can I pick just two songs for a bloke, when music was such a big part of his life? I want to do him proud, and I know it would have meant a lot to him, so I spent an afternoon in his garage trying to pick the perfect songs. I don't sit in his chair, I just can't do it. I flick through the vast collection of records he's accumulated over the years. After much deliberation, I choose, "Well I Wonder" by The Smiths to come in to, because I know it was his favourite. And for the retort, I choose "Tank Park Salute" by Billy Bragg. It's a song about a son saying goodbye to his dad. Speaking of the garage, Mum has decided she's keeping it exactly the way it is. Her exact words were, "I don't need to build a shrine for your father because he built himself one." Mum also tells me I need to let Michelle know. She was a big part of the family for so long and it's only right. I message her and once again I get nothing back. The worst part is, I don't even care. I return to work on Monday. When I walk through the office, people whom I've probably only said 2 words over the years come up to me and offer their condolences. It feels really strange, and I just want to get to my office as quickly as I can. By mid-morning, I've had a visit from Steve, welcoming me back, and Andy and Paul both come to visit me to see how I am and tell me if there's anything they can do to help, to give them a shout, Which I appreciate. I switch my computer on and when it's done firing up, I get a few email alerts. Mainly spam. My phone buzzes on my desk; it's a text message from Tiffany. It reads:

Hi Rob, how are you? What's it like being back in London? Are you missing Rome yet? It definitely isn't the same without you. I had such a good laugh working with you. Now I'm back at the office and I'm bored. Just to let you know, the advert is scheduled to start shooting on the 26th of May. I will send you another email closer to the time when I know the actual time and location. See you soon x

I re-read the message a few times, and it made me smile for the first time in days. I open up a blank message and for a while, I contemplate telling her about my dad. Then I remember the night we sat around the fountain, and she told me about her mum. I type out a message.

Hi Tiffany. I've been better. My dad passed away on the Sunday we got back to London, so I've only just returned to work. Rome was amazing. I still can't believe we got paid to basically go on holiday for a week. That's good news about the advert. See you soon.

After a while, I get a message back.

Oh, Rob, I'm so sorry to hear that. You must be devastated. I know from the way you spoke about your dad how much he meant to you. I hope you're holding up ok. Xx

For the rest of the day, I distract myself with work and ring Mum at dinner to make sure she's ok.

The night before the funeral, I stay at Mum's, and Jason does too. I'm so much more relaxed around him. Don't get me wrong, not all is forgiven, but the resentment I had for him is starting to soften. Mum makes us a curry, and we sit and eat at the dining room table. Even though there are three of us, it feels so empty without Dad. We settle down for the night and put a film on, but no one is really paying attention to it. Mum has an air bed blown up in the spare room, which is where I'm sleeping, and Jason takes the sofa. I lay there for ages dreading the next day. I don't get much sleep.

The next morning, we are once again sitting around the dining table. Mum has made tea and toast, but nobody has much of an appetite. Fortunately, the service is at 10:00 am, so we don't spend the whole morning pottering around, looking at the clock. When it's time, I put on my shirt, black tie, trousers, and shoes. I don't have a car. Mum doesn't drive, and we can't exactly go to the funeral in Jason's Ford Mustang, so we take a taxi. When we arrive, my initial thought is that we've accidentally crashed another funeral, seeing how many people are here. But Mum recognizes most of them.

The number of people I don't know who come up to me and tell me how they know Dad is unbelievable. I look amongst the crowd and there she is. Tiffany is standing with Andy, Paul, and Shelly. I can't believe she's here, but I'm so happy she is. I walk over to the three of them. She gives me a hug, and I smell her perfume. She always smells so nice.

"Thank you for coming," I say to her, and I really mean it.

"You don't think it's weird, do you?" she asks.

"Not at all, I'm pleased you've come. Why would it be weird?"

"Well, I've never met your dad, but I wanted to be here for you, really, for some support."

"Thank you," I smile. We go inside and take our place in the front row; the other rows fill up behind us. "Well, I Wonder" by The Smiths plays, and Dad is brought in and placed on the catafalque. The priest takes his place and begins, "Welcome everybody, we are here to celebrate the life of Graham Swan. The family has asked for their son, Robert Swan, to deliver today's eulogy." I walk up and take the place of the priest. I can feel a lump in my throat already, and I haven't even started talking yet. I take a deep breath and look around the room. I catch Tiffany's eye, she smiles at me.

It calms me a little, And I begin:

"You never quite realize how well-liked a person is until you see this many people attending their funeral. I've had so many people, most of whom I've never seen before, come up to me today and tell me how much of a great man my dad was. If there is an afterlife and he's up there somewhere watching this, I think he will be very pleased with the turnout. Because that's all anyone can ask for really. To have people who you've probably not spoken to in years come to pay their respects and share a memory or a funny story of a time you had together. You didn't even need to have known my dad very well to know that he loved music. This is the man who loved music so much that he sold his first car for £300, just so he could go see The Cure in France. He was also the guy who registered for Glastonbury tickets every year, and when he didn't get selected, he said it was rigged and wasn't bothering next year. His knowledge of music was so deep, he didn't just know the artists, he knew the names of all the band members and what pets they had. When we are kids, I wouldn't say we are selfish, I would say we are ungracious. We are totally oblivious to how much our parents sacrifice for us. We don't realize how much things actually cost or how hard they had to work to get them. And it's not until you grow up that you realize all you want from your parents is for them to be present. Just to show up when it matters, and my dad was there for everything.

Birthdays, Christmas, sports days, school, college, university, the day I passed my driving test. We went out to celebrate. He was my best friend, and I'm going to miss him. Goodbye, Dad."

There's a silence, and the priest comes back towards me, and I move to the side. "Now Graham's other son, Jason would also like to say a few words." Jason gets up and passes me as I make my way back to the pew. I look at Mum before I sit down, and she gives me a look as if to say she's just as confused as I am. I'm really nervous about what he's going to say. What if he starts ranting about being the black sheep of the family or saying bad stuff about dad? He clears his throat, And another lump forms in mine.

"There are a few things I never said to my dad while he was alive that I really should have," he starts. *"I never told him I'm sorry. Sorry for the pain and stress and worry I constantly put him through. Sorry for not realizing how great he was, and sorry for not getting to know the type of person he was, so we could have bonded a lot more than we did. The other thing I should have said is thank you. Thank you for giving me chances, even though I didn't deserve them. Thank you for never giving up on me, even when I was at my very worst. because you could quite easily of walked away Dad, but you didn't. if you had, I might not have been standing here today. Thank you for giving me the best life, that I've completely taken for granted. I love you, Dad."*

When he finishes, I don't think there's a dry eye in the whole place. He walks back and sits next to me. I put my arm around him, something I haven't done since we were really small. "I'm so proud of you," I whisper to him, and I really am. He mouths a thank you. Tank Park salute plays as the coffin is guided into the cremator, and people start to make their way out. We have the wake at **mum's house**. Everybody eats finger food and shares the best memories of Dad. Jason doesn't touch a drop of alcohol all afternoon; he sticks to tea. I'm standing talking to Andy, Paul, and

Shelley, and I notice Tiffany is talking to my mum. They are chatting away for a good half an hour, and I really worry about what my mum is saying to her. Hopefully, she has spotted the wedding ring on Tiffany's finger and thinks twice about embarrassing me. When Tiffany finally wrangles free, she heads to the toilet, and Mum makes her way over to me.

"I like her," she says, a little bit tipsy. "Very pretty, very down to earth." When Tiffany comes back, Mum tells me I should show her the garage. So I take her outside.

"Oh wow, this is incredible." She says, mesmerized. The weight of the day falls on top of me, and I'm fighting back tears.

"Oh Rob, come here," she says, putting her arms around me, and that tips me over the edge. I feel comfort in her embrace as the tears glide down to my cheeks. When she pulls away, she looks at me, and once again her face is inches away from mine, but this time it's different. In Rome, I felt desire. This time, I feel love. And I know it sounds silly, but I feel like we could stay in this room, just the two of us, for the rest of our lives, and I'd be okay with that. When I met Michelle, we were just kids, and it was young love. But this, I've never felt this before. The things my dad said to me in the hospital about living my life, finding the things that make me happy, and doing them every chance I get. Well, I want to do those things with Tiffany so badly that it hurts. I want to travel the world with her. Take romantic strolls across sandy beaches. I want to try the most famous foods in the most famous cities. And see the most iconic monuments. And it pains me to know it's never going to happen.

"Your dad would have been proud of you," she says. As I'm snapped out of my thoughts, reality comes crashing down on me. "Thank you," I say.

"Shall we go check on your mum?" she says. We leave the garage and go back inside. A lot of people have gone and after another half an hour or so, there's only me, Mum, Jason, Andy, Paul, Shelly, and Tiffany left. They stay to help us clear up. Then they leave too.

When it's just the three of us, we go to the garage and put one of Dad's records on, sit together, and celebrate the man who gave his all for us.

19. Lights, Camera, Boring

Monday 26th May 2025

We are in a studio in Manchester, getting ready to watch the filming of the first part of the advert. It's the scene where the actor is getting ready for his date and he puts on the aftershave. They've put us in a hotel that's within walking distance of the set. I thought we were going to rent out an apartment, but no, it's all being done on a set, the whole thing. I have to say I'm a little disappointed. I thought watching an advert being made would be really exciting, but it's a lot of standing around while the actor is in makeup and the cameraman sets up the perfect angles for the shots. We got to meet the actor, and he's nice. You can tell he's at the early stages of his career, where he's still raw and not used to the attention. Andy asks when the advert is going to be aired, and we are told they will have it all wrapped up by Friday, and the advert will air on Saturday night during primetime TV.
"They really aren't messing about, are they? That means most people in the country will see it," Tiffany exclaims excitedly. The concept of that is too much for us to comprehend. This is big, really big. At lunch, the cast and crew break for an hour, so the four of us do the same. We go to a little Mexican place around the corner and get a table for four.
"Rob, do you want to share nachos with me?" Tiffany says, taking her jacket off and putting it on her chair.
"Yeah, that sounds good to me," I reply, wondering why she asked me and no one else.
"While we wait for our food," Andy speaks, "I've got a scenario for you. Would you rather go to prison for five years for armed robbery, no one gets hurt but you have to do the full five years or go to prison for one year but it's for murder?"
"First of all, where the hell did that come from? And secondly, why is murder fewer years than robbery?' I say, confused.

"I read it somewhere this morning, and because it just is," he laughs.

Tiffany thinks about it before saying, "Depends on who I'm murdering. If it's someone everybody hates, then I'm a hero."

"It's not, it's a national treasure. Everyone in the world loves them. And when you're out, you can't walk down the street without people throwing quiche at you."

"Quiche. why quiche?" Paul laughs.

"It's the first thing that came to my head."

"Well, I'm taking the 5 years," I say. "I couldn't imagine murdering somebody."

"Anyway," Paul says, moving the conversation away from death and shooting a look at Andy. "I've got some news. Me and Shelly are getting married." Andy nearly spits his drink out. "I know what you're going to say. We've only known each other 9 months, and it's all a bit fast, but we already live together, and everything we've done so far has been fast, so why not."

"Paul, that's amazing. Congratulations," Tiffany says coyly.

"Yeah, congratulations mate," Andy and I say together.

"When is it?" Tiffany asks.

"June 26th," Paul replies, grabbing a menu. "At least you've got a year to plan it," Andy says.

"No, not June 2026, June the 26th this year," Paul laughs. "I know it's only a month away, but it feels right to us. Obviously, you're all invited. Will you be back in Rome by then, Tiffany?" he asks.

She thinks for a minute. "I don't have to be, and I'd love to come."

"What about work, though?" I ask hopefully.

"Well, if there's one thing 2019 taught us, it's that we live in a technologically advanced world, where, as long as you have access to a computer or laptop, you can pretty much work anywhere. I'll just work from my hotel room. Besides, when I'm back home, I never go into the office; I just work from home, so it won't make much difference anyway."

"Won't your husband mind?" Paul asks when she's finished.

"No, a few more weeks won't hurt. Plus, I think we could do with some time apart," she laughs, but there's a hint of realism in her voice. For the next half an hour or so, we talked about the wedding. Paul asks Andy to be the best man, which was inevitable really.

The next few days are pretty much the same as the first. The novelty of being on a set wears off very quickly, and it's actually really boring. Now and again, they will ask us questions on whether or not we are okay with certain parts of the advert, but other than that, we are just sitting around watching. I'm just thankful it's not a film set that drags on for months. When Friday comes around, we are told it's the last day of filming, and the four of us are so relieved that when the director calls a wrap on the whole thing, we don't even go to the wrap party. We are so desperate to get back to our own beds, that we catch an earlier train back to London. I feel sorry for Tiffany, Who checks herself into yet another hotel.

We are told that the advert is going to air at 7:12 pm on Saturday night, during this brand new game show (which, by the way, Paul didn't invent) because most people will tune in for it, With it being new and might be good. Mum asks me if I would like to watch it with her and tells me to invite Tiffany, Andy, Paul, and Shelly and She'll put a little spread on. Everyone thinks it's a great idea and that it makes sense for us all to be together anyway.
So the four of us, accompanied by Shelly, get the tube to Watford. We sit, eat, drink, and talk about how a year ago, none of us aside from Paul and Andy even knew each other. And how it's crazy that in the last 12 months, we've bonded over a project that is finally finished, and we are about to watch all that hard work come to an end in a 30-second advert. We all, nervously and excitedly, keep an eye on the time. And when it gets to 7:00 pm, the game show starts. It's two teams who battle it out in a series of physical activities. It's like gladiators, but instead of facing the gladiators, the teams just

face each other. At 7:11 pm, it cuts to the adverts and the six of us sit there in anticipation.

There's an advert about wash powder and then a car advert, and then ours starts. There's a dead silence as our eyes are fixated on the TV. We watch as Poised by Amato is introduced to the world for the first time. The advert seems to fly by, and even though we've seen it being made, it looks so much more authentic on TV. I would have loved it if we got some sort of on-screen credit, but obviously, that doesn't happen with adverts. When it's over, we are all like kids who have just come back from holiday, discussing our favourite parts. We raise our glasses and toast the efforts we've all made to make the advert possible. Tiffany catches me looking at her, and she smiles. The game show is still on in the background, and on the 3rd set of adverts, it's on again. Steve wasn't joking when he said they were going all out. We all watch it again. I've got a sneaky feeling I'm never going to get bored of seeing it. 10 minutes after the advert has aired for a second time, Paul is on his phone. 'OH MY GOD,' he shouts. Everybody stops their conversations and turns to him. 'I'm on social media and listen to this.

@Grantphelps49: *Did anyone manage to catch the name of the aftershave they've just advertised on ITV? The advert where the young lad proposes to his girlfriend.*

@stephanie_thomas: I think it was called Amato, I could be wrong.

@colinpotter: *It was called Poised by Amato.*

@Grantphelps49, thank you.

"And there's loads more," Paul says excitedly.

@shanecarter: *Finally, a decent aftershave advert, @Amatoaftershave.*

@blades123: *"Poised" by Amato is an aftershave advert that actually makes sense.*

@violet_parker: *Congratulations to Amato for making an advert that has so much meaning to it.*

@samnthajones: *That new aftershave advert, "Poised" by Amato, really pulls at your heartstrings. I'm a sobbing mess.*

By 8 o'clock, it's gone viral, and everyone is talking about it. There are a few negative reviews saying the advert is too cheesy, but other than that, it gets such a good reception. I go into the kitchen just for a moment to be alone. Mum follows me in and sees me looking a bit heavy-hearted. "What's the matter?" she asks, concerned.
"Just thinking about Dad, he would've loved this."
"I know, darling," she says and places her arm around my shoulder. It's such a strange feeling when a person you usually share all your joyful moments with isn't there anymore. It's like having a secret that you can't tell anyone. Since my dad died, I've been thinking a lot about all the things he's never going to get to experience. Little things like the end of TV shows he was in the middle of watching, the music he's not going to hear because it hasn't been released yet, and what the world's going to be like in 10 years' time. And then there are the more important things. Like how his family members' stories end. Did he die wondering how Mum was going to cope without him? What does the future hold for me and Jason? Did he die hoping me and Jason would start talking again? Maybe he already knows. Maybe he's seen everything that's happened since that day, and tonight he's sat and watched all of us celebrating something to be proud of. I sure do hope so.

20. Embarrassment Killed The TV Star

Monday 2nd June 2025

The following Monday, I arrive at the office. As I walk in, I'm expecting thunderous applause from everyone. Like a scene from a film where a hero returns to work after saving someone's life from a burning building, and the whole office just stands and claps. But what I actually get is 'Morning Rob' from 2 people, and the rest just nod at me. I make myself a cup of tea in the shared kitchen. As I'm taking my mug out of the cupboard and putting a tea bag in it, Steve walks past, looks in, and then realizes it's me.
"Ah, there you are," he says like he's looked everywhere for me. "First of all, I just want to say great work. And secondly, have you ever seen the morning show with Brian Claymore?"
"A few times, why?" I ask, pouring scalding hot water into my mug.
"Well, his representatives have been in touch, and they want two members of the team who were heavily involved in the making of the advert to go on the show on Wednesday. They are doing a bit on the advert. Now, obviously, I've chosen Tiffany, as she is the manager of the bigger branch and took the lead on the project. I asked her to pick someone to go on with her, and she was adamant it had to be you. So, get yourself ready for Wednesday because you're going on TV," he says nonchalantly. This has to be a wind-up, surely. Any minute now, I'm going to see the hidden cameras, and he's going to shout 'GOT YOU,' but he doesn't. He just turns around and walks off. I get to my office, sit down, and try to get my head around what had just happened. Me on TV. I'm not sure that's a good idea, I'll be shitting myself. At 9 o'clock, I get a text message from Tiffany.

Rob Swan, this is Tiffany Murray from the magazine, Television Weekly. I'm doing a segment on people's rise to stardom, and I wondered if I could arrange an interview with you so our readers can really get to know TV sensation Rob Swan and what really makes him tick. X

I send her a reply.

Ha-ha, I think you've made me even more nervous now x

You have nothing to be nervous about. I'm a pro. Any chance you could meet me at the cafe around the corner during your lunch hour, and we will make a plan for Wednesday? X She replies.

Yeah, sounds good to me. I think I'm going to need it x
I write back.

I get to the café, and Tiffany is already seated. I order a cup of tea and a cheese and ham panini. As I walk over, Tiffany smiles at me, and it hits me that I need to appreciate that smile because soon she will be gone, and I will never see it again. I take the seat opposite her.
"So, when you said you were a pro, what exactly did you mean?" I ask before taking a bite of the panini.
"I was in a theatre production of 'Grease' just after I left school," she replies, coolly.
"What the West End?"
"No, it was only an amateur production," she answers.
"Did you get much of an audience?" I ask.
"No, it never got made. The company ran out of money."
"That hardly makes you a pro," I laugh.
"Yeah, but what I'm saying is, I'm used to being in the spotlight, so if you want, I will do all the talking."
"That's exactly what I want," I say, relieved.
"Right," she begins. "The show starts at 6:00 am. We are not on until 8:00 am, but it's still going to be an early morning. The studio

is in Waterloo, so it will only take about 15 minutes to get there. Meet me here at 6:30 am, and we will get the tube together. Does that sound like a plan?" I nod and take another bite of my panini.

Tiffany is either bored, lonely, or genuinely likes my company because she could have told me the plan in a text message. Not like I'm complaining, I really enjoy spending time with her. She takes a sip of her tea and It's then that I realize she's not wearing her wedding ring. Wait! Was she wearing it at the funeral? Obviously, I was too preoccupied to notice. Maybe she just took it off to wash up or something and forgot to put it back on, and then came to Manchester without it. I can't read too much into this; it's probably just a coincidence. I also realize that I'm not going to get many more opportunities like this to tell her how I feel about her. Of course, I can't tell her how I really feel because she's married (well, I think she is) and that's not fair. But I want her to at least understand how fond of her I am.

I can feel my cheeks turn crimson as I start, "Tiffany, I just want to say thank you again for coming to my dad's funeral. It really did mean a lot to me. Can I also just say it's been a pleasure working with you this last year. When Michelle left, I was in a slump and really didn't know what to do with myself. Paul and Andy have been brilliant, but you've kept me smiling even when I had nothing really to smile about." She smiles at me again. "Rob, you are a genuine, nice guy, and that is so fucking rare. Believe me, I know. You've had a lot of shit happen to you that you really don't deserve. But unfortunately in life we make choices, and the rest is down to luck. You deserve to be happy, and I honestly think you will be. It's been such a pleasure working with you too. Promise me we will keep in touch when this is all over?"

"Of course," I reply. I look at the time and realize my dinner is nearly over. "I better get back to the office. See you Wednesday," I say before leaving.

I meet Tiffany at the cafe. Despite it being June, it's too early to be warm and I regret not bringing a jacket. She walks up wearing one, and I envy her. Underneath her jacket is a polka-dotted blouse topped off with blue jeans, and she looks as stunning as ever. I can't help but think she will look even better next to me, who looks like someone has put a shirt on a scarecrow. We get a pot of overnight oats and a cup of tea before getting the tube. It's early, so it's nice to have a carriage to ourselves. We arrive at the studio, a big burly man guards the door. Tiffany shows him the email she received that gets us in. We are greeted by a woman wearing a Bluetooth headset and we are told to follow her.

  She takes us to a dressing room and tells us to take a seat in the makeup chair, which I think is quite condescending. It's like she's saying that we've done a shitty job making ourselves look presentable for TV, so here are some professionals to make you look less shitty. After the first, and hopefully the last, time I have makeup put on my face, we are TV-ready. They take us out and stick us behind a camera, which is pointing to Brian Claymore, who is currently talking about a new cookbook that's coming out. Once that segment is over, he stares straight down at the camera and begins, "Now, let me ask you this question: When you see an advert on TV, do you have any idea who the masterminds behind it are? I know I don't. Well, my next guests are the creators of the advert 'Poised' by Amato. If you haven't seen it yet, where have you been? Because it's all over every social media platform and it's only been out since last Saturday night. So, I'd like to welcome to the show Tiffany Murray and Rob Swan." I take a big, deep breath and follow Tiffany past the camera, and onto the sofa that's 3 feet away from Brian's.

Brian: *First of all, welcome to the show.*

Me: (very nervously) Thank you for having us.

Brian: *Now tell us, how did you come up with the idea for the advert? And what made you go in that direction?*

Tiffany: Well, unfortunately, Brian, we live in a world where society has set the bar far too high. People are told they are too ugly, too fat, too skinny, too old, too young. So we thought that if we went with an advert (bearing in mind this was our first advert) of a Hollywood actor on a beach, shirtless, exposing his perfect body. We're not really helping people's perceptions of how we are apparently supposed to look. And we know it sounds cheesy, but we want people to see our advert and know that no matter how they look, our aftershave is for them. We want people to spray it on, smell nice, and feel confident wearing it. In regards to how we came up with the advert, we actually stumbled across it when a young man proposed to his girlfriend in front of us on a business trip. (Brian laughs) It was then Rob (she points to me when she says Rob) who started the idea rolling and we went from there.

Brian: So, how long have you been working on this? And how big is the team behind it? Is it a big team? Or just a few of you? Because too many cooks spoil the broth, type of thing.

Tiffany: We've worked on it since last June, so around about a year. And the team, believe it or not, is only 5 people. There's myself and Rob. Then there's Paul Fields and Andy Parks, who both played their part massively. We couldn't have done it without them. Additionally, the project was overseen by Steve Smith, the boss of the London branch.

Brian: So, what was the secret to successfully putting it all together as a team? Like, how did you agree on things?

Tiffany: Well, I would have to say honesty. Instead of just agreeing with each other, we weren't afraid to shoot down an idea if we weren't quite feeling it. At the same time, there were no stupid ideas. We were all brave enough to put one out there, even if it wasn't the right one.

Brian: Now Rob, we've not really heard from you. How would you describe your relationship with the team? Did you already have a close working relationship with these people, or did that materialize over time?

I want to do a Tom Cruise on The Oprah Show. Jump up and down on the sofa, proclaiming my love to Tiffany, but decide against it. Instead, my cheeks burn, and I realize I have to be careful here and keep it professional. I can't let my emotions get the better of me.

Me: Before we started, I obviously knew my boss, Steve. And I knew Paul and Andy, who were both brilliant at making everyone feel welcome and were both real assets to the project. Tiffany, I'd never met before, but I'd heard she was good. And I have to say, her reputation exceeded her. She was professional and driven, and for someone who had never met any of us, she fit in straight away from day one. I know the others won't mind me saying this, but she led the project, and it wouldn't be half as successful without her.

I can hear my brain saying *'Shut up now then, Rob.'*

Me: She's a great asset to any team.

My brain comes back. *'Seriously, Rob, shut the fuck up.'*

Me: 'I have no doubt that she's going to carry on doing great things.'

Brian: Brilliant stuff. I think we can all agree it's a fantastic advert. Thank you once again for coming on, you two. Ladies and gentlemen, Tiffany and Rob.

We exit the set and step outside onto the pavement. "Sorry," I say. "I got a little carried away in there. I didn't mean to embarrass you, I just....." She kisses me. It happens so fast, and I'm not at all expecting it, so I don't kiss her back. I don't even move my mouth. I just stand there like an idiot. It's like she's giving CPR to one of those dummies on a first aid course. She pulls away.
"Fuck, I shouldn't have done that," she says, turning away from me.
"Tiffany, it's fine. I didn't...."
"Shit. Shit. Shit. I really shouldn't have done that. I've got to go Rob." She walks away, leaving me on the street of Waterloo, dazed and confused.

21. You've got to fight for your right to party!

Friday, 6th of June.

I haven't seen Tiffany since she kissed me. I sent her a text that night.

Tiffany, I'm not going to tell anyone what happened. Just forget about it, and we can go back to normal. I would hate for things to be weird between us, and I really don't want the last few weeks before you go home to feel awkward.

I decided against putting a kiss at the end of the message.

It's Friday, and I still haven't had a reply from Tiffany. I haven't texted her since because I don't want to bombard her or put my foot in it even more, if that's what I've done. Around 11 o'clock, Andy knocks on my office door.
"Alright mate, do you have a minute?" he asks.
"Yeah, sure," I reply while pressing send on an email.
"Don't tell him, but on Friday, I'm throwing a stag do for Paul. He thinks we are all just going out for a meal, which we are, but after that, we are going to tell him it's his stag night, Are you up for it?"
I think about it for a minute, with what's going on with Tiffany. It's probably what I need because if I don't go, I'll sit at home moping and staring at my phone, hoping she will text me.

"Yeah, I'm in," I finally reply.
"Tonight, at our usual Indian restaurant at 7:00. Don't wear a shirt," he smiles. He leaves, and I'm left wondering why he doesn't want me to wear a shirt.

I put on a casual T-shirt and jeans before leaving the house. It's a nice night; there's no wind, so the weather's warm. I take the tube to Holborn. When I enter the restaurant, I follow the stairs down to the seating area. I must be one of the first ones here because there's only Paul and Andy sitting at a table. Then I realize we are obviously meeting the rest of the people Andy's invited later; otherwise, Paul would know something's going on. I take a seat, and the waiter comes over to take our orders. If we are going out after this, I don't want to overdo it, so I order a few small plates instead of a big curry. When Paul skulks off to the toilet, I turn to Andy. "Are we meeting everyone else after this?" I whisper, even though Paul is well and truly out of earshot.
"Yeah, we are meeting Steve in a bar down the road," he whispers back.
"What, just Steve? Is that it? A four-person stag!"
"We don't really know anyone else, and Paul hasn't got any brothers," he says, **animated**.
"Besides, he won't mind. He doesn't even know he's having one."
Paul returns, and the food comes out, and we chat in between bites. After we finish eating, we pay the bill and leave.

We walk towards a bar called Juice, which sounds like a smoothie bar.
"Shall we nip in here for a drink?" Andy says hopefully.
"Nah, I should be getting back to Shelly," Paul replies. I realize that I've now got to help persuade him.
"Come on mate, just a quick one. I've got something I want to tell you both anyway," I lie. He gives in.
"One drink, and I mean one as well,"

We go in. The bar is in the middle with tables everywhere. There's a DJ booth in the corner. Music blares around the room. Steve is seated at the bar with a pitcher of beer and four glasses. When he sees us coming, he pours the beer into the glasses and motions to the barman, who hands him a carrier bag.
"What is this?" Paul asks, surprised.
"IT'S YOUR STAG NIGHT!" Steve yells. And he's clearly been drinking without us. Andy takes the plastic bag off Steve and hands me a policeman's shirt and hat, gives one to Steve, and keeps one for himself. He then hands Paul an orange jumpsuit. He holds it up. "I don't get it?" he questions.
"You're a prisoner, and we are the policemen because it's your last night of freedom," he laughs, and thankfully, so does Paul. We all put the outfits on. Steve struggles to get his large shirt over his even larger frame.
"One more thing to complete the setup," Andy laughs, as he pulls out a pair of metal handcuffs. "Hold your hands out." Paul obliges and Andy handcuffs his hands together. We find a table and sit down.
"Wait a minute, does Shelly know?" Paul asks.
"Of course, she knows," Andy laughs, "it was her idea."
After a few more drinks and laughing at Paul trying to lift his glass up with handcuffed hands. We get on to the subject of work. Well, not work, more the advertisement and what it's going to mean for the company. Steve tells us that pre-order sales for Poised have gone through the roof, and that's just pre-sale. He predicts that when the aftershave actually hits the shops, it's going to be way bigger than we ever expected. Of course, I'm excited, but I'm also really apprehensive. It's a feeling of elation and worry, like someone who wins a lot of money feels. You want it to happen, but you're scared of just how much it will change your life. On a table to the left of us is a group of women. It doesn't look like they are out for a special occasion; they just look as if they are out for a typical Friday night. One of the women comes walking over. She has

blonde hair and brown eyes. She's wearing a black dress with the biggest high heels I've ever seen. She towers over our table as she leans on it.

"Are you guys on a stag night?" she slurs.

"What gave it away?" Steve asks sarcastically.

"The fancy dress," she replies before realizing and faking a laugh.

"Where's the rest of you?"

"They are all on the dance floor," I reply, trying to make us sound less pathetic.

"Do you guys want to play beer pong with us?" she asks, which was the reason she stumbled over in the first place.

"Yeah, we'll play," Andy yells, answering for all of us. I mentally check the bucket list of things I didn't necessarily want to do but ended up doing anyway.

- Hotdog eating contest.

- Football match.

- Blind date.

- Speed dating.

- Appear on a morning TV show.

Oh yes, there it is. play beer pong with four drunk strangers. So once again, off I go to a table that's got 20 cups, 10 on each side, in a triangle formation filled with god knows what. "Basic rules," says one of the women whose name, like the rest of them, I have no idea. "If you throw a ball and it lands in a cup, the person on the other side of the table has to drink whatever's in that cup. Right, let's play," and that was the rules over with. Andy goes first and gets it in, showing that unlike me, he's probably played this game before. Then it's Steve who throws it, but it goes wayward and is closer to hitting the DJ than one of the cups. Then it's my turn and I'm not much better.

The woman I'm up against gets it in. I pick the ball out of the cup and down the clear liquid. It tastes like a paint stripper and almost takes the enamel off my teeth. Forget going to the dentist for a deep clean; they should just give you a shot of this. Then it's Paul's turn.

"Can I take these handcuffs off?" he shouts to Andy.

"No, you aren't taking those handcuffs off. They cost me a tenner," Andy shouts back. It gets to a point where there are 3 cups left each. everybody except Andy and the blonde woman has lost interest and given up. One of the women sits down next to me. She tells me her name is Hannah. "I've just worked out where I've seen your face. You were on TV the other morning, you've got a new cookbook out," she yells over the music.

"That wasn't me," I yell back.

"No, it definitely was. I never forget a face," she says adamantly.

"No, I mean I was on the show, but not for having a cookbook out."

"Why were you on the show then?" she asks.

"I helped create an aftershave advert."

"Oh my god! The advert where the man proposes to his girlfriend. I love that advert. It's amazing. Do you have any free samples?" She shouts. Why I would bring samples of aftershave out with me? I'd never know.

"It's not out yet," I shout back.

She puts her hand on my leg, "You're like a celebrity," she teases.

I can see where this is going and I don't want it. As soon as she touches me, I think of Tiffany. Because if anything is going to happen between us, which I doubt it will considering she's not even talking to me. I'm not sure she would appreciate me getting

together with some woman I met on a makeshift stag do. I tell her I need the toilet, which isn't a lie because I do. On the way to the toilet, I check my phone, but still nothing back from Tiffany. When I come back, I ask Andy if we can go somewhere else and luckily he agrees that it's time to move on. The next bar we go to is a karaoke bar. A woman is on stage butchering "Simply the Best" by Tina Turner. We find a table as far away from her as we can. After a few more drinks, I can feel myself getting to that point where I'm going to regret it if I don't stop. Steve, on the other hand, isn't letting up. Just as I think he's about to go to the bar to get us all another one, I'm saved. "NEXT UP ON THE KARAOKE: STEVE, PAUL, AND ANDY," the man next to the stage shouts. And for once, I can sit back and watch the chaos instead of being thrown into it. They make their way to the stage and Steve shouts, "KICK IT," into the microphone, and we all watch as two blokes dressed as police officers, and one dressed as a prisoner, drunkenly annihilate "Fight for Your Right to Party" by the Beastie Boys. When they return to the table, I tell Paul that I'm ready to call it a night, and I'm surprised when they both say that they are too. We tell Steve we are going, and he announces he's staying, so the three of us leave. The fresh air hits me and knocks the wind out of me a little bit, and for a second I think I might heave. I place my hand on a wall and double over. Paul places his hand on my back. But nothing comes out.
"Are you okay, mate?" Andy asks.
"Not really," I reply.
"I have something I need to tell you." They both give me their full attention.
"I'm in love with Tiffany," I say. And it's out there; I've told them. They both burst out laughing. "What's so funny?" I ask, confused.
"We already know that," Andy howls.
"What do you mean, you already know?"
"Mate, it's blatantly obvious" he smirks.
"How long have you known?"

"Since day one. Put it this way, you haven't hidden it as well as you think you have," Andy continues to laugh.

"Do you think she knows?" I ask, panicking.

"Of course she knows, she's not stupid. In fact, she's the complete opposite of stupid. But unfortunately for you, she is married," Andy finishes.

"What am I going to do?" I say pathetically.

"There's not really a lot you can do," Paul exclaims.

"That's life, I'm afraid. A lot of the time we want the ones we can't have. Life is full of shit timing and bad judgment. Now, I don't know about you two, but I'm hungry," he finishes. We spot a chip shop which remarkably is still open at 12:30 am. As we walk in, there's a bit of a queue, so we join the back of it. A small dumpy woman shouts over the counter at us. "Do you guys want anything cooked?"

"Yeah, all of it," Paul shouts back. She stares at him confused. "What do you mean by all of it?"

"I mean, I want it all cooked, not just some of it. I don't just want the fish cooked, do I? What am I going to do with uncooked chips? I haven't got a deep-fat fryer at home."

"Actually, I'll leave it. I'm not that hungry anyway," he says, annoyed. We leave the chip shop, and the three of us go our separate ways. When I get into bed, my mind is a whirlpool of emotions. But it's mainly confusion. I try to work stuff out from what I know.

-Tiffany isn't wearing her wedding ring.

-She told Paul she could come to the wedding and that she and her husband could do with some time apart.

- According to Paul and Andy, she knows I'm in love with her.

-She kissed me, but she said she shouldn't have done it.

That really didn't help at all. I'm more confused than when I started. I check my phone again, but still nothing from Tiffany. It takes every fibre of my being not to text her. After what feels like an eternity, I drift off to sleep.

22. And the winner is ...

Monday 9th June

In a full calendar year, there are a lot of days to celebrate: Mother's Day, Father's Day, Easter, Valentine's Day, Christmas Day. Days like that. And then there are the ridiculous ones: World Hypnotism Day, International Hot and Spicy Food Day, and International Sweatpants Day. And that's just in January. So when Steve calls me, Andy, and Paul into the conference room to tell us that there's an award ceremony for the best television advert and Poised by Amato is nominated, I'm not shocked that the award ceremony exists, but I am shocked that we've been nominated.

"How have we been nominated? The advert has only been out for two weeks," Paul says, confused.

Steve explains, "The cut-off point was Monday 2nd of June. So any advert that aired before that date was considered. Our advert was reviewed by a panel of judges who looked at."

- Creativity
- Innovation
- Impact
- Design
- Copywriting
- Use of the medium
- Memorability

"And it's made into the nominees. So get your tuxedos hired. We are going to an awards ceremony," he finishes excitedly.
"When is it?" I ask.
"Wednesday 18th June," Steve answers, checking the email on his phone. The ceremony is in a hotel in Croydon, so we will be spending the night in the hotel. When I get back to my office, I decide it's time to text Tiffany again. I still haven't heard anything from her, and it's been over a week. I get my phone out and type a simple message:

"Great news about the award ceremony, isn't it?"

About an hour later, she actually writes back.

"Yeah, it's amazing. I can't wait for it."

At least she's replied, I think to myself as I carry on working.

On Sunday, I go to visit Mum and tell her all about it. She's over the moon for me and tells me she recorded me on TV. I tell her I've never watched it back, not even once. It will only remind me of what happened after. "Do you want me to put it on?" she asks excitedly. "No, thanks, mum. So, how have you been anyway?" I ask, changing the subject.
"I've been alright, darling. The book club girls have been keeping me company, and I've been doing a lot of knitting recently. By the way, your brother is coming out on the 4th of July," she says, as if he's just done the last 5 months in prison.
"I'm going to do a little homecoming for him, on the 6th. Nothing big, just a barbecue for the three of us. What do you think?"
"Yeah, that's fine," I reply. I stay for dinner. Mum makes us roast chicken with all the trimmings.
"Oh, I forgot to ask you," she begins, pouring gravy all over her dinner.

"Do you want your dad's golf clubs? I don't know what to do with them."

I haven't got the heart to tell her that I'm not really going to play golf without Dad. "Yeah, I'll take them," I smile, and it seems to please her. The way I see it, what's not going to ruin my day might make hers. She tells me that instead of me lugging them around on the tube, she will get Jason to drop them off once he's home. The way she says "home" tells me that this is where he's going to be staying, but I could be wrong. I say my goodbyes and make the journey home.

On Monday, Steve takes me, Andy, and Paul to be fitted for a tuxedo, and better yet, the company is covering the cost. When we get to the place, I'm a little bit disappointed to learn that none of the tuxedos have been rented out by famous people. It would have been really cool to wear a tuxedo that's also been worn by a red carpet A-lister. Once we've all been measured up, we choose our tuxedos. Because there's no spending limit, I go all out and choose a full tuxedo, which includes: a jacket, trousers, shirt, waistcoat, bow tie, and pocket square. As I'm trying on my tux in the mirror, I think about the ceremony. Tiffany will be there, and I'm hoping I get a chance to talk to her properly. Although getting her on her own might be tricky, with her avoiding me.

It's the day of the awards ceremony, and we have to be there at 2:00 pm. The awards aren't on until the evening, but we have to go through some sort of rehearsal. I have a shower and throw on some casual clothes. Our tuxedos are being sent to our hotel rooms. Because getting to Croydon from King's Cross is a bit more difficult, with there being no tube line that goes there, Andy offers to drive the four of us. Well, he actually offered to drive the five of us, but Tiffany said she would make her own way, which does not bode well for tonight's events. I hear a beep outside my window, and I pull the net curtain aside to have a look. Steve sits in the passenger's seat. He motions for me to come, and I leave the house. The drive to Croydon is about an hour, depending on traffic. I take my seat in the back next to Paul. On the way, we talk about how amazing it would be to win, especially as we are up against some big-name adverts like Coca-Cola, Apple, and Google.

As we get closer to Croydon. I feel a fluttering of nerves. Not for the awards; that doesn't bother me. I'm nervous about seeing Tiffany for the first time since the show. When we get to the hotel, I spot her waiting for us in the car park. She says hi to all of us and shoots a nervous glance at me before turning away. I just don't get it. For as long as I've known her, she's never struck me as the shy type in anything she's done. I think back to how confident she was on the set of the morning show. It was like she was born for it, and now she's completely gone back into her shell. Steve checks us in at reception before handing us our key cards. Mine is room 504. Four of us are on level 5, and Tiffany is on level 7, after we've checked out the rooms. We go back downstairs to the lobby. A man shows us to the table we are sitting on and we all take a seat. I want to sit next to Tiffany but we've all got assigned seats. I'm in between Andy and Paul, then it's Steve, and then Tiffany is, unfortunately, the furthest away from me. The host takes the stage; she is a woman with long black hair and a glittery black ball gown. She tells us how it's going to work. There are 8 awards, ours being the last one. Meals will be served before the show starts so people won't be eating and then have to get up halfway through if they win. She tells us the bar is now open and that everyone is expected to be at their tables by 6:00 pm. This gives me four hours to try and talk to Tiffany. I would hate for the ceremony to start with any bad blood between us.

"Steve, I will come with you to get everybody some drinks if you want," she says, getting out of her seat. Steve follows. This is going to be harder than I thought. And it is. Every time I try to get her attention, she's started another conversation with Steve. The time ticks by far too quickly. I look at my watch, and it's 5 o'clock. We are all going to start getting ready soon, and I still haven't spoken to her. I decide to concede defeat. I'm sitting at the table with Andy and Paul. Tiffany is at the bar again with Steve, laughing. I wouldn't say she was drunk, but she's well on her way.

"Fuck this, I'm going to go get changed," I say to Paul and Andy.

"We are going to finish these, then we will as well," Paul replies, lifting his glass up to show me he still has half a pint. I walk past the bar.

"Where are you going, Rob? Don't you want another drink?" Steve asks.

"I'm going up to get ready, so I'll skip the drink," I reply. As I walk past, I catch Tiffany's eye; she looks at me sheepishly. I take the lift up to level 5 and scan my card in room 504. I shower, shave, and put my tux on. I'm not arrogant in any way, shape, or form, but even I have to admit this is the best I've ever looked. My beer belly has gone from months of running, and the tuxedo fits me perfectly. I spray on the aftershave that got us to this moment; *Poised by Amato*. We all received a bottle last week before it officially hit the shops. There's something about wearing an aftershave that I helped produce, and the public can't have yet, that makes me feel good.

I check the time; it's 5:15 pm. I hear a knock at the door. I curiously open it; it's Paul and Andy. "We have to tell you something," Andy says excitedly.

"I can feel my heart rate quicken."

"Tiffany isn't married," Paul blurts.

"What? You mean they've split up?" I ask.

"No, she never was married, and there's no boyfriend either."

I am so confused. "How do you know this?" I can hear my voice getting frantic.

"She just told us that she lied about the whole thing," Paul explains.

"You know what this means," Andy almost yells, "go for it, mate."

But it's not as easy as that. Because they don't know about the kiss or the fact that she's not talking to me. One thing is for sure, though. I need to talk to her.

"I'll go talk to her now," I tell them, and they both leave smiling. I check myself in the mirror before exiting my hotel room. I walk down the hall towards the lift and press the button. The lift comes to a stop and the doors slide open. I step inside and press the number 7. The doors close and the lift whirs upwards. As I step off onto the 7th floor, I can feel myself shaking a little bit. I take a deep breath. As I walk down the hall, a door opens and I hear voices. I recognize the voice straight away. I look down the hall and that's when I see my boss, Steve, coming out of Tiffany's hotel room.

I quickly double back on myself and walk past the lift and around the corner before he sees me. I hear him press the button for the lift. His breathing is heavy. The lift arrives and the doors slide open. He gets in and presses the button; the doors close, and the lift drops and my heart goes with it. I take a slow walk down the stairs to level 5 so I don't bump into him. I open my room with the key card and drop down on the bed. It all makes perfect sense now. She made out she was married so no one would suspect that her and Steve were together. No wonder she got chosen for the job; he probably hand-picked her. And all those nights she wouldn't come out with me, Paul, and Andy were because she was with him. No wonder he was gutted when he couldn't come to Rome with us. And all that bullshit about her husband working nights and needing some space from each other. And when she kissed me and said that she shouldn't have done that, it was because she didn't want Steve to find out. I feel so stupid. I sit there in silence, my mind is a washing machine of emotions. Oh well, it's like Paul said, there's nothing I can do about it. I just need to go down there like nothing's happened. I grab the key card off the side and make my way downstairs. When I get into the lobby, the place is heaving. It's almost like a coach full of people has just suddenly turned up. I enter the function room and get a drink from the bar; I order a whiskey and coke. Paul, Andy, and Steve are already seated. I take my seat in between Paul and Andy. Tiffany walks through. She's wearing a long red evening gown, her hair is slightly curled, and she looks stunning. She orders a glass of wine at the bar. As she walks over, I try not to stare. She takes her seat next to Steve.

At 6:30 pm, they bring the starters out; I've gone for French onion soup. I look over and see Tiffany and Steve laughing together. I know they aren't, but it feels like they are laughing at me. My main course comes, and it's fillet mignon and mustard mash, and it's probably one of the best things I've ever tasted. My dessert follows soon after, and it's warm chocolate fudge cake and ice cream. I'm a bit full, so I **don't** finish it. After they've cleared the plates, I whisper to Paul and Andy to meet me outside. We pick up our drinks and exit the hotel. "You've got to be fucking joking," Andy says after I've finished.
"I'm sorry mate, that's awful," Paul adds.
"At least, I know now," I say dejected. We head back inside and retake our seats. About 15 minutes later, the host takes the stage and the awards ceremony begins. We sit and drink through the many categories: Best social media advert, best radio advert, best billboard advert, that kind of thing. It finally gets to our category.

"Now, ladies and gentlemen, it's time for our final category: Best television advert. Here are your nominees: Coca-Cola. The big screen shows a snippet of each advert: Google, Apple, Hyundai, and Amato's."

"And the winner is..." My heart is in my mouth.

"COCA-COLA," she yells. We all look at each other, gutted but trying so hard not to show it.

"A toast," Steve says, raising his glass into the middle of the table. I really don't want to clink glasses with him, but as a team, we deserve to celebrate what we've achieved. So I stick my glass in the middle. "Amato's," Paul says, and everyone mimics him.

After a couple more drinks, Steve is the first one to call it a night and leaves the table, and coincidentally, 10 minutes later, so does Tiffany. Watching her leave is like a dagger through the heart. I decide I'm no longer in the mood, and I say goodnight to Paul and Andy.

As I walk through the lobby, I see Tiffany outside, sitting on a bench on her own. I decide I deserve an explanation, so I make my way out to her. She sees me walking over, and she smiles at me for the first time all day.

"Mind if I sit down?" I say. She nods.

"So, Steve then," I say, smiling at her but dying inside.

"What about him?" She asks confused.

"You and him are together, aren't you?" I ask.

"STEVE!," she laughs. "You must be joking, aren't you? What gave you that impression?"

My heart is going like an Olympic sprinter.

"Well, Paul and Andy told me, that you had told them, you weren't married. So, I came upstairs to talk to you, and I saw him coming out of your hotel room." She laughs so hard, I think she's going to fall off the bench.

"Steve came to my hotel room because he never got a bottle of champagne in his room like he requested for all of us, in case we won. He wanted to see if I got mine. You, Andy, and Paul were still downstairs at the time."

"So why did you tell everyone you were married when you weren't?" I ask.

"Rob, I was about to lead the biggest project of my career with three single men. I had to keep it strictly professional. If everyone thought I was married, then everyone knew where they stood, and we could just focus on the job at hand," she answers.

"You really think a lot of yourself, don't you?" I tease, making sure she sees me smiling. Thankfully, she smiles back. "Come on, though, Rob. You can see where I'm coming from, can't you?"

"I can," I admit. "So, when did you realize I was in love with you then?" I ask, because at this point, what have I got to lose?

"To be honest with you, I realized quite early on. Paul and Andy were the same every day. But you weren't. You were a lot more reserved around me. It was like you were worried you would say something that I didn't like, and that's when I knew." I look at her sheepishly. She continues, "I didn't feel the same way until much later," she says. It takes me a moment to realize what she's said.

"You feel the same way?" I ask, alleviated.

"Of course I do," she replies, as if it was blatantly obvious. "Why do you think I opened up to you about my past and none of the others? Why do you think I was adamant that you come on the show with me? I even sent you a message saying Rome wasn't the same without you."

"So when did you start feeling this way?" I ask apprehensively.

"The night of the gig, when we ended up going to the hospital, I started to feel it. And then you bought me breakfast, and we got to know each other properly, and it just got stronger from there."

I'm trying so hard to contain my excitement because we are not done yet. "So what happened outside the studio of the morning show then? You kissed me and then started panicking and saying you shouldn't have done it."

She looks at me like she's about to give me bad news. "Because you never kissed me back, you just stood there, and I never should have done it, because it had only been 2 weeks since your dad had died and there's me kissing you. So I panicked and ran, and then I started thinking maybe I've got this all wrong and you didn't feel that way about me. And when you texted me telling me to forget about it, I thought I'd truly fucked it up. So I kept a low profile from you, knowing that I would be going back home soon. Because I couldn't stand being rejected, not after everything."

I look at her and I can't believe how wrong we have both got it. "It all happened so fast and my brain didn't comprehend kissing you back. And I thought you were saying you shouldn't have done that because you were married. So that's why I said to forget about it because I didn't want you to get into trouble."

She laughs at me. "This is my fault, isn't it? I got so caught up in pretending I had a husband that I didn't really take into consideration what that meant for you. The thing is, Rob..." I don't let her finish; I lean over and kiss her properly. This time, my mouth moves, and so does hers. It's the most passionate kiss I've ever had. It lasts for about 20 seconds, and when she pulls away, she smiles at me. Then, she takes my hand, and we are almost sprinting through the lobby to the lift; she presses the button. Every second the lift takes I think she's going to change her mind. When the doors open we step in and she presses 5, I look at her. "Yours is closer," she whispers. The doors close, and we kiss again. When the doors reopen, we move quickly down to room 504, and I fumble around in my wallet for my key card. We enter the room, and I finally do something that I've done so many times in my head over this past year. I spend the night with Tiffany Murray.

23. His name is Alan

You know when you wake up in an unfamiliar place, and it takes you a while to realize where you are, and the events of the night slowly make their way back to you? That's what happened to me the following morning. At first, I think I dreamt of spending the night with Tiffany, then I saw her red gown on the back of one of the chairs. But she isn't here. I think maybe she woke up this morning and regretted it, and left, but accidentally left her dress here because her little clutch bag is gone as well.

Luckily, before I start to feel a bout of self-loathing coming on, I hear the door click and she walks in carrying two cups of tea in takeout cups. I breathe a sigh of relief. She places one of the cups down next to the side of the bed I'm currently lying in. "Morning," she says, smiling and kisses me. Her mouth tastes of stale alcohol and tea, but I really don't care, and it appears she doesn't either because she does it again. We sit for a few minutes sipping our tea. As we do, the thoughts of what this means for us run through my head, and I know we are going to have to have a conversation about it at some point. But for now, I'm just enjoying the moment.

When it's time to make a move, she goes back to her own room, and I jump in the shower. I put on my casual clothes and head down for breakfast. When I get to the table, Paul and Andy are already there. How early do these two get up?

"Morning, mate," Paul says, with a smug smile slapped across his face.

"Good night?" Andy adds, and has the same look.

"Yeah, it was good," I say, smiling back.

"I bet it was," Andy sniggers. And then it strikes me that they know.

"So, I take it you know then," I say, failing to smother my smile.

"Yeah, we saw her coming out of your hotel room this morning,"

I tell them the story while Tiffany and Steve aren't there, and when I finish, they laugh. When Tiffany and Steve eventually join us, we talk about the award ceremony and how we all feel about not winning. None of us are too disheartened about it. It's been a crazy year, and we're all just happy to be mentioned in the same breath as these massive companies. Once we've finished breakfast, nobody is in any rush to leave, so we stay around the hotel for a bit. After about half an hour, Tiffany says she is going to her room for a lie-down. Five minutes later, I get a text from her.

"*Come to my room X.*"

I tell the rest of them that I'm going to lie down as well. Paul and Andy give me a look that says they don't buy it one bit. I reach Tiffany's room and knock on the door. She opens the door and leads me onto the bed. We have sex again. This time, it's even better because there's no alcohol involved, so it's 100 times more intimate. When it's finally time to leave the hotel, we say goodbye to Tiffany. She was going to jump in with us, but the company had paid for her return train ticket, and she didn't want to waste it. In the car on the way home, I think about texting her but decide not to be too eager; I'll wait until I get home. We haven't even been gone 10 minutes when my phone buzzes. And it's Tiffany.

I can't wait to see you again xxx.

Me neither. Will you be my date for Paul's wedding? Xxx.
I type back.

I see the little dots moving so I know she's typing.

I thought you would never ask xxx.

She replies:

Thursday 26th June.

It's the big day. Paul and Shelly's wedding. I've spent every night with Tiffany since the night of the awards ceremony. With her flight back to Rome being on Saturday, the 28th of June, two days after the wedding, we are trying to spend as much time together as possible. We went to the cinema, gone out for meals, and spent a lot of time at my house. The best thing about it is how comfortable and easy it is between us. That's the benefit of knowing someone for a full year before getting together; there are no awkward silences. I also feel that I can fully be myself around her now, and she seems to like it.
I'm all dressed and ready. I'm wearing navy blue trousers with a white shirt and a navy blue tie. It's far too warm for a blazer, but I take it anyway. Tiffany arrives, and she's wearing a khaki green, Bodycon Wrap, Midi Dress with Long Sleeves. She looks absolutely gorgeous.
We arrive at the church and spot Andy, so we go over to say hello.
"Where's Paul?" we ask.
"He's around the back of the church, and he's a nervous wreck" Andy smiles. Paul appears a few minutes later, and he looks as white as a sheet.
"Good luck," I tell him as we make our way into the church and take a seat in one of the pews at the back. Paul and Andy take their places at the front. You can see the sweat on Paul's face a mile away. When the church is full, the vicar greets Paul and Andy. The deafening sounds of the organ play the wedding march and Shelly appears at the door in her wedding dress with a ridiculously long train. We all stand as she strolls down the altar to take her place alongside Paul. The vicar tells everyone to sit and begins the ceremony.
"Dearly beloved, we are assembled here in the presence of God to join Paul and Shelly in holy marriage, which is instituted by God,

regulated by His commandments, blessed by our Lord Jesus Christ, and to be held in honour among all men."

After more discussion about all things religious, the vicar asks if anyone present knows any reason why these two people shouldn't be married. I don't want anything bad to happen to this wedding, but I can't help thinking how funny it would be if someone burst in holding a really old document and said, "You can't marry Shelly; she's your cousin," or if a woman burst in saying, "Stop the wedding! That's not Shelly Cooper. I'm Shelly Cooper." Obviously, nothing like that happens, and the vicar continues. After Paul and Shelly promise to look after each other in sickness and in health and all the other stuff, they put on the rings, kiss, and everybody celebrates. We watch as they leave in a horse and carriage, before following them down the road to the reception.

At the reception, we take our allocated seats amongst the many tables that all face one big long table for the bride, groom, best man, and parents of the newlyweds to sit at. The starters come out. I've gone for Blue Cheese and caramelized onion tart. I help myself to the free wine and pour Tiffany a glass. The main course is beef wellington and mash, and for dessert, I have a white chocolate creme brulee. After all the food has been cleared and wine glasses have been topped up with champagne, it's time for the speeches. Shelley's dad speaks highly of his daughter and promises to really hurt Paul if he ever hurts her, which sounds aggressive, but it was all done in jest. Paul then does the standard groom speech, thanking everyone for coming and saying how beautiful his new wife looks.

And then it's time for Andy's best man speech. He takes the microphone off Paul and stands up. He looks nervous. He opens his jacket and takes out a small piece of paper. "First order of business," he begins. "Can the owner of a horse and carriage please move it? It's blocking the entrance." Laughter fills the room and Andy relaxes.

"For those of you who don't know me, I'm Andy. Paul's best man, which is clearly obvious, otherwise I wouldn't be standing up here with a microphone in my hand. I've known Paul since school, which is a very long time. the only way I can describe Paul is Barry and Paul chuckles long-lost brother. He's ditsy but very lovable with it. I mean, this is a bloke who thought he was buying a Yamaha motorbike for £150, didn't read it properly, and was devastated when the bloke turned up with a Yamaha keyboard. He thought he was getting a right good deal. Sorry Shelley, but good luck is all I can say. The bloke never fails to make me laugh. We went through school together, college together, and university together. We even lost our virginities together. I don't mean we slept together or took part in a threesome. I mean it was on the same night. (More laughter) He's gotten me through life, and there is no man I would rather have had by my side. Now … Shelly and Paul met at a speed dating night, which I also took part in. So technically, I could say I dated her first. Joking aside, though, she is perfect for him, and we can all agree she looks stunning today." Shelly feigns blushing by waving her hand in front of her face. "But what is love?..

There's a long pause. "By the way, this isn't the start of some sentimental quote. I'm asking you all a question because I have no idea. I think love is finding something like what Paul and Shelly have and watching it grow. And I can't wait to watch it grow with them. So without any further ado, I would like you to raise your glasses to the happy couple. To Paul and Shelly!"

"To Paul and Shelly," everybody repeats.

Once Andy's speech is over, it's almost like a pilot removing the seatbelt sign on an aircraft. Everyone gets up and roams around, drinking, talking, and laughing. About half an hour later, we are asked to turn our attention to the dance floor where Paul and Shelly are about to have their first dance. David Gray's "This Year's Love" plays, and the couple sway from side to side. Once the song is over, it's open season, and the dance floor starts to fill up. Tiffany, who is ever the extrovert, takes my hand and leads me onto the dance floor. She takes my hand and I follow her lead.

"You're amazing," I say, and she smiles. "No, I mean it. Before I met you, I wouldn't have done any of the things I've done in the last year. You have this amazing ability to make me want to try the stuff that would normally scare the shit out of me." The room starts to fill up with people who were only invited to the reception.

We are still dancing away together when I see a woman sitting at a table staring at us, and then I realize who it is. It's a heavily pregnant Michelle.

I have to look again to make sure, but it's definitely her. What is she doing here? Who even invited her? I tell Tiffany that the woman who's been giving us daggers for the last 5 minutes is Michelle.

"So what? Let her stare," she replies, pressing her hips up against mine. After a few more songs, we take a break from dancing and return to our table. Michelle never takes her eyes off of us. I can't help but keep glancing over to see if she's still looking.

"Go and talk to her," Tiffany says. "Get it over with; you won't be able to enjoy the rest of the night until you do." She's right, I won't. I get up and make my way over to the table she's sitting on.

"Hi," she says, smiling, but I'm not.

"Can I talk to you outside?" I say.

"Sure," she replies, getting out of her chair and following me.

"What are you doing here?" I ask when we are out of earshot of a group of guests who are sitting at a table outside. "You don't even know anyone here."

"Yes, I do," she counters. "Shelly and her mum used to come to the cafe all the time. I used to tell you about her when you would ring me from Cambridge." It doesn't ring a bell at all, but she must be telling the truth because why else would she be here? "Anyway, you've moved on quickly, haven't you?" And I realize she's talking about Tiffany.

"You're the one who wanted to move on, and speaking of moving on, you're not really one to talk," I say, pointing to her stomach. "I see you got your one-night stand with a Frenchman, what was his name, Pierre?" I ask bitterly.

"No, his name is Alan, actually."

"That's not very French," I reply.

"He's not French, I met him in France when I went to stay with Mum. He's from Kent, and he was on holiday."

"So you've not been travelling around the world then?" I ask.

"No, I stayed at Mum's for the first six months while I waited for Jennifer to come to France. Then I found out I was pregnant in October. When I told Alan that he was going to be a dad, he asked me to move to Kent with him, and I've been there for the last 6 months." I want to laugh at the irony of it all, but a thought occurs to me. She's been less than 50 miles away for the last 6 months.

"Did you know my dad died then?" I ask, but I'm sure I already know the answer.

"Yeah, Mum told me."

"So, you didn't think to maybe show up and pay your respects, since you'd known him for 12 years?" I ask.

"I thought the last thing you'd want is me there." She's right, I didn't want her there, but I don't tell her that. "Do you hate me?" she asks after a small silence.

"I did when you first left, but it got easier, and then good things happened to me inside and outside of work," I reply honestly.

"I saw the advert and the morning show. Congratulations, Rob."

"Thank you," I say sincerely.

"So what's her name then?" she presses.

"Her name's Tiffany,"

"And are you happy?"

"Yeah, I really am. If you'd asked me that 3 weeks ago, it might have been a different answer, but yeah, I'm very happy."

"Are you?" I ask.

"Yeah, definitely," she exclaims. "I'm so excited to become a mum, to a boy or a girl, we haven't found out yet. It's funny, isn't it?" she continues. "After 12 years of being together, we both seem happier away from each other." I think she's right. But again, I don't want to tell her because it would mean her leaving was the right call, and I can't give her that satisfaction.

"Right, I'm going to go back inside," I say, stretching. "I'm pleased we had this talk; it finally feels like closure. Good luck with everything, Michelle," I give her a hug. When I get back to Tiffany, I tell her what happened and she smiles smugly before dragging me back onto the dancefloor.

As the night is coming to an end, she asks me to take a walk with her. We exit the venue and take a slow walk around the botanic gardens. There's an air of silence as we walk side by side, and I wonder which of us is going to break it.

"It's been a really good day, hasn't it" I say finally.

"Yeah, it's been lovely, way better than my wedding," she laughs.

As we carry on walking, I spot a bench next to a fountain surrounded by garden lights. We sit for a bit. I stare at her in admiration. Time is running out. I need to know what is going to happen, but I'm scared of the answer. She finally spots me staring.

"What is it?" she says, smiling.

"Are you going to talk to Steve about getting a transfer?" I ask, instantly regretting the abrasiveness of the question. She looks as though I've shattered her heart.

"I can't do that, Rob. Steve is the manager of the London branch, and I've worked so hard to become a manager. My career is in Rome. I was hoping you would transfer and come back with me," she replies desperately. I sit there for a few seconds and think about my answer.

"I can't leave Mum, not after Dad's just died," she goes quiet, and I think she's going to change her mind.

She sighs heavily. "Well, then at least we had this one good week," she says, and I realize she's crying. Despite the warm night, her words are like ice.

"Don't say that, we can make it work. What about long distance?" I'm desperate now. This can't be the end, it just can't be. It's only just getting started. Again, she mulls this over. I'm hoping she's trying to figure out a way for this not to be it.

She finally speaks. "It wouldn't work, Rob. In this past week, we've spent every day together." I know she's right, and for the first time, I hate that she is. I desperately cling for this not to be the last time I see her.

"I can still see you before you go, though, can't I? We still have tomorrow." I plead.

"I'm sorry, Rob, but it's going to be too hard to say goodbye to you for good." Her face is now completely soaked. "I think we should say goodbye now," she replies.

My heart sinks. She takes her phone out and orders an Uber. We sit side by side on the curb, she rests her head on my shoulder, and I can smell her shampoo. I occasionally kiss her head. She follows the little car on the Uber map. When he's 1 minute away, we both stand up. She leans in and kisses me. As she pulls away, I see another tear roll down her cheek, smudging her mascara. I take my thumb and wipe it away. The driver arrives, and she opens the door before getting in. She waves to me, and I wave back half-heartedly as the car pulls away.

24. Christmas in July.

It's been 10 days since I said goodbye to Tiffany, and every day has been worse than the first. I so desperately want to message her, but I know it will restart the healing process all over again. I try to throw myself into work, but it's hard when every part of the place reminds me of her. I think about the day I first met her in the conference room. The way my heart beat out of my chest when she first walked through the door. Her smile reduced me to mush. I remember that same night when I watched her humiliate a drunken idiot who tried to hit on her. And that was the moment I realized she was hilarious. I remember the moments in that same conference room, where she showed us all just how smart and forthcoming she was. I think about the night of the gig, I'd never been so pleased to have dislocated my shoulder. I think about Rome and the morning show. I think about the award ceremony and the pure joy I felt when she told me she felt the same way. Sharing our first proper kiss, waking up, and her bringing me tea, it was probably the happiest I'd been for a long time. And finally, I think about how she looked so stunning all the time, that I was envious of everyone she spoke to that wasn't me. I really have no idea where to go from here.

Sunday 6th July.

It's the day of Jason's homecoming, and I'm on the tube on my way to Mum's. Coincidence plays its part again, as Moby's "Why Does My Heart Feel So Bad" rings in my headphones. When I get to Mum's, the smell of burnt charcoal fills my nostrils. I walk through and out to the garden; Jason is tending the barbecue. He sees me and raises the plastic tongs to say hi. He looks bulkier than before, but he looks healthier with it. The smell makes my stomach grumble. I sit and talk to Jason while I watch him turn the burgers over. When the food is cooked, we sit at the outside wooden table as it's a nice warm day. We sit and listen to Jason talk about rehab, but it's not in a conceited way. Mum tells him she's proud of him, and I tell him I am too and that he's done really well. He thanks us but tells us the hard part starts now.

"Mum showed me the morning show interview," he says smiling. I cringe a little. "It was really good, You should be really proud Rob." It's still strange hearing him speak so mild-mannered, and take an interest in someone, or something that's not about him. Me and mum stick to soft drinks because we don't think it's fair to Jason. It's not really going to help his sobriety to watch us chug back alcohol. We sit, talk, and eat and I'm surprised when the subject of Tiffany doesn't come up especially when I told mum everything. Mum has a sixth sense about these things when I spoke to her on the phone last week she could tell something wasn't right. After we've finished eating we clear the tables and pack the barbeque away.

Jason and Mum go inside. I go into the garage. Dad's urn sits on one of his shelves. I sit in his chair. It still smells of him. I've found myself talking out loud when I'm on my own recently. I don't know if Dad can see me or know what I'm thinking, so if I talk out loud it's my way of talking to him, So if he is listening, he knows how I'm feeling. "Hi, Dad. I really miss you. I could really use some of your advice. I really want to go to Rome and be happy, but I can't leave Mum and Jason. It's not fair. What if Jason relapses? I don't think Mum is strong enough on her own to deal with that, not after everything that's happened. I don't know what to do." I'm not really sure what I'm expecting to happen; he's not going to answer back. I suppose I will just have to carry on with things the way they are. Eventually, I go back inside. Mum has made me a cup of tea.

"I think you should give Rob his Christmas present early," she says to Jason.

"Christmas present? It's July," I ask confused. He opens one of the china cabinets in the dining room and hands me an envelope.

"You are going to want to open this now," he says excitedly. I carefully tear open the envelope and inside is a one-way first-class ticket to Rome.

"What's this?" I say, my heartbeat quickening.

"Me and Mum have had a long talk and we think you should go to Rome."

"But...," I start to say.

"Don't worry about us," he interrupts. "We will be fine, won't we Mum?" Mum nods. I can see she's starting to well up. "I'm going to move in with Mum, and we are going to lean on each other until we get sick of each other," he laughs.

"But how can you afford this? You've not been working, and you've just had to pay for rehab," confusion filled my face. "I sold the car. Didn't you notice it wasn't in the driveway?" With everything that's gone on with Tiffany, I hadn't noticed. "I got £65,000 for it," he says, like it's no big deal.

"But you loved that car," I say, not quite believing what I'm hearing.

"Yeah, I did, but if I'm going to live here, I don't even need a car really, do I? It would just be a very expensive garden ornament," he finishes.

"Are you sure about this?" I ask, close to tears.

"Of course we are sure, just promise us you'll visit every 6 months," Mum says, wiping a tear away from her cheek.

"Besides, we can't have you moping around here for the rest of your life, can we?" Jason adds, smiling. I finally get the tongue-in-cheek banter you're supposed to have with your siblings.

I smile back. "Thank you," I say, throwing my arms around Mum before doing the same to Jason.

"Thank you, Jason. I really appreciate this." When it's time to say my goodbyes, I thank them once again. And I go home to pack.

Epilogue.

Chicago, one year later.

"Oh my god, that is the best pizza I've ever tasted," Tiffany exclaims, taking a very generous bite out of an authentic deep-dish plain cheese pizza pie, as they call it over here.
"Say that again for our viewers who didn't quite hear you," I say into the camera.
"Did Tiffany Murray just say that was the best pizza she's ever tasted and it wasn't a pizza from Italy?"
"Try it," she says, sticking the melted cheesy slice in my face. I take a bite and have to admit, I can't argue with her.
"No, she's right," I say. "That is unbelievable." The camera stops rolling.

Allow me to explain.

It was past midnight when I arrived in Rome. I didn't tell Tiffany I was coming; I wanted it to be a surprise. When I got there, I took the metro to the Trevi Fountain and sent her a message.

You are right, the Trevi Fountain is beautiful, but it would be a lot better with you here. Why don't you come and join me? Xxx

When she arrived, it was just like it is in the films where the guy shows up at the airport at the end and waits for the girl to get off the plane. She sees him and they embrace. I know that is unbelievably cheesy, but after all that has happened, I felt like I deserved that ending.

I moved in with Tiffany and for the first couple of months, I worked at the Rome branch of Amato's while she continued to work from home.

But just after Christmas, our lives changed.

Once the actual product *Poised*, was released to the world, it became popular and gathered a lot of attention. The advertisement for it became one of the most watched adverts ever. Many of those same people then went back and watched the interview with Tiffany and me on the morning show. Despite not regularly checking her social media accounts, Tiffany started gaining a large fan base that she was completely unaware of.

After Christmas, we took a trip to Sweden and Tiffany decided she wanted to try Swedish meatballs from various restaurants and rank them from worst to best. She shared her experiences on her social media pages. Now, I know the internet is a powerful platform, but I had no idea just how influential it can be. Her video received millions of shares and countless views, greatly aided by the fact that we had previously been seen on TV. It got so much traction that we were approached by a television company that thought Tiffany's confidence in front of a camera was just what they wanted for their show, which was a half an hour a week show, of someone (Tiffany) going around different parts of the world and trying out lots of different restaurants and whittling it down to a top ten, so holidaymakers who were going there would know where's best to eat.

Tiffany had one stipulation: that they let us do it together, which they agreed to. I was skeptical at first, but Tiffany said that she would drive and I could just sit in the sidecar, which I was more than happy with. That was in February, and so far we've done Seattle and Atlanta, and now we are in Chicago. This is what Paul meant when he said being credited in the advert would open up so many doors for us. Speaking of which, I should probably tell you how everyone else's story ended.

- Steve died in a speedboat accident.

- Andy lost all his money gambling on the stock market.

- Paul is doing time for tax fraud.

- Jason ended up getting together with Michelle and is helping her raise her baby.

Only joking. Could you imagine?

- Steve remained the boss of Amato's.

- Andy became a sports journalist.

- Paul stayed in advertising but managed to finally create his own game show, which is doing really well.

- Jason went to college to become a mechanic and moved out of Mum's.

Speaking of Mum, Tiffany and I have decided that we don't need to live in Rome anymore, considering that we no longer work there. So, we are moving back to London once the first series of the show has finished shooting.

We return to our hotel room after a long day of sampling Chicago's finest restaurants. We brush our teeth and climb into bed.
"Rob, when we move to London, we will have to start going running, otherwise I'm going to be the size of a house with all this eating."
"Yeah, I think we will have to," I reply.
"Goodnight, Tiff. I love you."
"Goodnight. I love you more."

The end.

Printed in Great Britain
by Amazon